ALSO BY PARKER GREY

GET DIRTY
Boss Me Dirty
School Me Dirty
Ride Me Dirty
Double Dirty Mountain Men
Double Dirty Royals
Rule Me Dirty

FILTHY FAIRY TALES
Finding His Princess
Waking His Princess
Protecting Their Princess
Claiming His Princess

ROUGH & RUGGED
Her Obsessed Mountain Man
Her Rock Hard Mountain Man

STANDALONES
Four on the Floor
Double Bosses
Action

D1736129

DOUBLE BOSSES

AN OFFICE ROMANCE

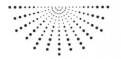

PARKER GREY

CHAPTER ONE

JENNA

"Ow!" I MUTTER AS SOMETHING SHARP DIGS INTO MY ELBOW, jerking my arm away from the edge of the bed.

Next to me, there's a small but annoyed snort, followed by a chirp.

"Okay, okay," I tell Gertrude, my very impatient cat.

She responds by putting one paw on my shoulder, then head-butting me right in the face. Lovingly.

"I'm getting up," I tell her, without opening my eyes. "I swear, every day you try this fifteen minutes earli—"

Mid-sentence, I finally open my eyes. In the half-darkness of my room, my bedside clock is glaring 8:35 in big, glowing green letters.

I rub my bleary eyes with one hand, because that's gotta be wrong. I went out with my best friend Sasha for her birthday last night, one drink turned into a couple, and I must be seeing this clock wrong...

Nope.

Now it's 8:36.

"Shit!" I yelp, and shove the covers back, accidentally flopping them onto Gertrude, who squawks in protest. I should be on the subway already, or at the *very* least, waiting for a train.

Definitely *not* still in bed.

"Sorry!" I tell her, already frantically running to my tiny closet and flinging it open.

That's when I remember that I was going to do laundry last night. But *then*, Sasha called from the bar down the street, and, well, now my already-slim professional wear pickings are even slimmer.

Muttering to myself, I grab a white blouse, a tan skirt I don't really like, and a pair of black pumps before turning for my underwear drawer.

Where my only option is the ridiculous magenta leopard-print push up bra Sasha made me buy a couple of months ago when I actually had a date for once.

The date didn't see the bra. I didn't wear the bra on the date. I didn't even see the date again, because even if he was an investment banker with a trust fund, he was *boring*.

I roll my eyes and put the bra on, dressing as quickly as humanly possible while Gertrude meows at my feet. I feed her, swipe some mascara over my lashes, drag a brush through my unruly strawberry blonde hair, and leave my tiny studio apartment in record time.

I get to the subway at 8:55. It's a thirty-minute ride, and then a five-minute walk.

I'm late, obviously.

When I finally get there, I open the big glass doors of Hamilton, Clarke, and Leonard as quietly and sneakily as I can, but it's hard to be subtle when you're opening an eight-foot-high door to a massive, perfectly polished lobby where people wearing thousand-dollar suits are already waiting.

Alicia, the receptionist, looks up at me and raises one eyebrow. She looks perfect, of course, because she always looks perfect: black hair neatly in place, subtle makeup applied near-professionally, headset perched on the side of her head.

I smile back, straightening my shoulders, trying to pretend like I'm late for a reason, like I had to... do some professional task on my way to work this morning.

Pick up a legal briefing? Sure, that's something I could have — in theory — been doing.

"Good morning, Jenna," she says coolly.

I smile back, haphazardly.

"Hi, Alicia," I say, forcing perkiness into my voice. "Great day, huh?"

Her eyes flick to the window. It's overcast and shitty outside.

"Lovely," she says.

I nod, heading down a hallway to her right so I can sneak to my desk the back way, through the break room and past the storage closet.

I duck into the break room. The coast is clear, so I head through to the door on the far left, trying to stay casual.

I open it, head out into the hall. The door to the supply closet is open, and I straighten my back, preparing to walk past quickly so that whoever's inside doesn't know it's me.

I'm halfway past when a powerful, slightly husky voice booms out from within.

"Jenna," it says with just the *hint* of a Southern drawl. "You don't happen to know which staples my stapler uses, do you?"

I freeze.

Shit.

Lawson Marshall, one of my bosses and a partner at Hamilton, Clarke, and Leonard, knows I'm late to work. Not only is he late to work, he probably went looking for me so I could get him more staples.

I clear my throat and back up a few steps, peeking into the closet, hoping that somehow it's not actually him, just his voice doppelgänger.

"We seem to have two different kinds," he says, looking down into his hands where he's holding two boxes of staples. "Did you know staples could be so flummoxing?"

He glances over, and just like that, my heart skips a beat, my stomach clenches, and other things...

...ahem.

Lawson Marshall, Esquire, has the sort of sandy-hair, blue-eyed, All-American charm that could have made him a movie star if he hadn't become a brilliant lawyer instead. As I stand there, trying to remember the question — *staples?* — he shoots me a smile that makes my toes curl in my shoes.

Stop it, I tell myself. *He's your boss. Just because he's hot as Hades doesn't mean he's flirting with you.*

Finally, I point at one box of staples.

"Those are for the big stapler," I say, suddenly at a loss as to what *the big stapler* is actually called. "You know, the one we have to use if we're making a booklet or have to staple a lot of pages together at once? Your office stapler uses the other one."

"I knew it had to be something," he says, casually putting the wrong box back on the shelf.

He takes a row of staples from the box and tosses it end-over-end into the air, then catches it casually.

"Much obliged, Miss McAlister," he says, turning the full weight of his gaze onto me.

I stand my ground and maintain eye contact, purposefully not looking down at the perfectly-tailored dark gray suit skimming his body, or the way he *obviously* dresses left.

Yes, I checked out my boss's dick.

I couldn't help it.

And I'm not sorry.

"You're welcome," I say, surprised to find my voice.

He walks toward me. I forget to move out of the way until he's almost up to me, flicking off the closet's light switch and throwing himself into momentary darkness.

"In fact," he says, his voice suddenly lower, an urgent note in it. "I'm so obliged that I won't even tell Kade you were tardy today."

Kade Chandler is my *other* boss, another partner in the firm who works closely with Lawson. *Really* closely; they're best friends as well as coworkers.

I've heard *other* whispers about them as well, but it's just secretaries gossiping in the break room. There's no way what those girls are insinuating could possibly be true.

And even if it were, what do I care? I'm their employee. Their personal lives are none of my business.

A prickle goes down my spine, and I exhale, hard. I hadn't even realized I was holding my breath. Lawson Marshall is a mere foot away from me, and I swear I can feel the animal heat rolling off him, something untamed, feral, *ravenous* beneath that well-fitting suit.

"Thank you, Mr. Marshall," I murmur.

"Don't mention it," he says.

Then he *winks*, and just like that, he's gone, striding past me and back toward his office while I stand there, trying to shake off what just happened.

Did something happen? Or was it just my imagination, because my boss is insanely hot and it's been a *very* long time since I got intimate with anyone.

Well, technically, it's been forever, seeing as how I'm a virgin. I've done *stuff* with guys, but I've never gone all the way.

If we're being honest, I've never gotten particularly far. I just haven't met someone who interests me quite that much yet.

According to Sasha, I just need to get on a dating app, pick a random hot guy, and swipe my v-card already, but I'm not that kind of girl. I can't just lose my virginity to *just some guy*, you know?

Lawson disappears around the corner, and I remind myself that I'm at work and need to stop thinking about anything sex-related at all, even if it's just the sad state of my own affairs, and get to work.

CHAPTER TWO

LAWSON

I leave my door open so I can watch Jenna walk to her desk. She's twenty minutes late to work, and although I know I ought to reprimand her for that, that moment in the supply closet more than makes up for it.

Even if I had to find my staples myself, because her rush to get here has left her flushed and breathless, cheeks pink, chest heaving. I can tell she was careless getting ready this morning because the bright pink bra she's wearing under her white shirt is perfectly obvious, and it complements the perfect swell of her ass and the pout of her lips *perfectly*.

Her hips sway as she walks with the unconsciously sexy stride of a girl who has no idea I'm watching hungrily. Instead she's glancing around the room of busily typing legal secretaries, looking at the clock, her hot-as-sin walk the last thing on her mind.

My cock swells in my pants just watching her. Good thing I'm already sitting, because partner or not, sporting a raging hard-on while watching your assistant get in for the day isn't a good look.

I've got rules, after all.

No fucking coworkers.

And *especially* no fucking my own assistant. It's against every single Human Resources policy we've got here. It flies in the face of the boring video on sexual harassment I have to watch twice a year.

If I did and I were found out? I'd be fired *instantly*, no questions asked. No chance to explain.

None of that stops my cock from getting even harder as Jenna bends down to put her purse into a desk drawer, and I involuntarily clench one fist and try not to think about the fantasies I've been having.

Fantasies of Jenna, bent over my desk, that tight pencil skirt hiked around her waist.

Jenna on her knees, hands on my thighs, as my swollen cock slips between her red lips and she looks up at me, pure hunger in her eyes.

Jenna sitting on my lap, riding my cock reverse cowgirl, my hands cupping her breasts as Kade stands in front of us, his cock in her mouth as she moans—

There's a quick knock on my open door as the man himself walks in.

"Have you seen the Abercrombie documents yet?" he asks. There's no prelude, no *good morning, how are you?*

With Kade, it's always straight down to business, and it always has been — at least since we met in law school eight years ago.

"I'm having a *lovely* day, and yourself?" I ask, grinning and leaning back in my chair.

At the desk outside my door, Jenna sits down quickly and gracefully, smoothing her hair as she waits for her computer to start up. I will my erection away.

Kade just rolls his eyes at me.

"Yes, sure, hi, good morning, how are you, I'm doing great,

birds are singing and shit— *Have you seen these discovery documents, Lawson?"*

I cast one final glance at Jenna, then sit up straighter and grab the file from him, tossing it onto my desk.

"Or are you too busy staring at your assistant to get any work done?" he asks, smirking.

"I've got no idea what you're talking about," I deadpan.

His smirk just gets smirkier, his voice lowering.

"So you weren't thinking about the way her tits would bounce when she rode you?"

"I was doing no such thing," I say evenly, lying through my teeth.

Kade knows I'm lying, and as I open the folder, he leans over my desk, his voice going even lower.

"You weren't thinking about shoving that tight skirt up over her luscious ass, bending her over your desk, and making her moan your name?"

Kade knows me way, *way* too well, and he sits on the far side of my desk, file in my hand totally forgotten. To anyone else in the office, it looks like we're just discussing a case.

"Or maybe you're just wondering whether she can handle both of us at once? It's been a while, Lawson."

I don't say anything, because the mere thought of both of us taking Jenna together — the way our assistant would scream and moan, the way her body would be absolutely wracked with pleasure — is making me hard as a rock underneath my desk.

And Kade is right. It *has* been a while since we shared a girl like that, made her lose all control. Months, almost a year, maybe.

Past Kade's form on my desk, my eyes alight on Jenna, totally oblivious to the conversation we're having. Just looking at the back of her neck makes a prickle of desire go up my spine.

Suddenly, I don't care how much trouble I could get in for having an inappropriate relationship with my assistant.

I don't care if this girl could get me fired.

I don't care if my best friend and I are out of a job this time next week. I want to see Jenna like that, out of her mind with pleasure as we both fuck her at once, those wide, innocent eyes rolling back into her head as she comes again and again.

I *need* that, consequences be damned.

"Tell me about the Abercrombie files," I finally growl at Kade, my eyes still on Jenna.

He just chuckles and opens the folder.

CHAPTER THREE

KADE

"Miss McAlister," I say, and Jenna jumps in her chair.

Even though I'm a big man — a little over six feet tall and a former college rugby player — I tend to walk quietly, and that means sometimes I sneak up on people without meaning to.

Jenna swallows quickly, turning in her office chair, then smiles slightly.

"I wish you'd just call me Jenna," she says, her big eyes looking up at me.

Fucking hell, she's gorgeous. Even worse, she's the kind of perfect, gorgeous girl who has no idea how beautiful she is, or the effect she has on men.

The effect she has on me, at least. I can barely walk by her desk without feeling the blood heat up in my veins, the near-irresistible desire to grab her like a caveman and carry her back to my bed crawling through me.

I want to do filthy, dirty, *unspeakable* things to Jenna. I want to own every part of her and show her pleasures she's never even imagined before.

And I know someone else who wants the exact same thing.

Now we just need to figure out how to go about this.

11

"If I just called you *Jenna* you might not know it was me," I say, my voice coming out a rough rumble even though I mean it lightly.

She blinks.

"I bet I would," she says. "No one else here really sounds like you. Did you need something?"

You, on your hands and knees, I think. *Or my face between your thighs, sweet honey underneath my tongue...*

I clear my throat.

"Have you been able to contact Judge Renfro regarding next week's hearing yet?" I ask, forcing myself to stop thinking about Jenna naked and think about my *actual job* for once.

Jenna's eyes flick downward. It's only for a split second, and then they flick back up so fast it could have been my imagination, but my cock twitches in my pants anyway. It's taking all my willpower not to pitch a massive tent right now, and she's making it ten times worse.

"I did," she says, reaching for a note pad. "She said that the hearing was scheduled for…"

Jenna gives me the short version of her conversation, and I force myself to pay attention to the boring, work-related words coming out of her mouth.

I'd rather pay attention to the way she rests her pen against her lip when she's thinking, the way her fingers are absent-mindedly playing with the hem of her skirt on her knee.

The effect she has on me is completely insane. It's unlike anything else I've ever felt, this assistant who I've shared with Lawson, my best friend, for a few weeks now.

That is, we've shared her assisting capabilities. We haven't shared her in any other capacity… yet.

But we're going to. I can feel it. Lawson wants sweet, innocent Jenna just as badly as I want her, and assistant or not, there's only one way this is going to end.

And that's with Jenna gasping with pleasure, screaming out our names.

"Mr. Chandler?" she says, and I realize I haven't listened to a word that's come out of her perfect mouth in minutes. I clear my throat and re-focus my attention.

"Kade," I correct her without thinking.

Jenna bites her lip for a split second, eyes dancing.

"Only if you call me Jenna," she says, her voice soft but teasing.

As soon as she says it, a pretty pink blush rises to her cheeks.

Jenna is *flirting* with me, even in our buttoned-up, very formal office.

I arch one eyebrow at her.

"Are you telling me what to do, Miss McAlister?"

Her blush darkens instantly, and her eyes flick downward again, though not to my cock.

"Of course not," she says quickly. "Sorry, Mr. — uh, Kade…?"

Sometimes I forget the effect I have on people, that I'm tall and built and according to Lawson, don't smile nearly enough. I know I make people nervous — especially sexy new assistants.

But I have to admit that she's pretty like this, flustered and pink. I wonder what she'd look like even more flustered and pinker.

I wonder what she'd look like if I told her what I'm thinking, right now — that I've got half a mind to tell her that I need to see her in my office, then shove her skirt over her waist and slide my fingers into her little pink pussy until she comes.

"Perfect," I purr at her, and I could swear she colors even more.

Just as she does, a door opens across the open-plan office floor, and Jack Leonard emerges, along with someone I recognize as Marshall Gale, the CEO of one of the largest investment firms in the city.

Jack glances around the room, his eyes flicking over me for a moment, but it's enough to remind me what's at stake here, and I straighten instantly.

If we're going to seduce Jenna — and we are — no one can know. *Especially* not the other partners at the law firm.

"Have that on my desk by noon," I tell her, straightening my tie out of habit. I barely even remember *what* I'm asking her to have on my desk at noon, but I'm sure she'll get it there.

Too bad I won't be having what I really want — *her* on my desk.

At least, not yet.

CHAPTER FOUR

JENNA

CALL ME KADE, HE SAID.

That's all I can think about for the next couple of hours as I prepare the report he asked me for.

Well, that and the tent in his pants. Hard not to look when he was standing, I was sitting, and that *monster* was right at eye-level.

Because good God, was it big. I may be a virgin, yeah, and I may be fairly inexperienced even for a virgin, but I've seen penises before. I've even seen big penises before — it's not like I've never seen porn.

But in real life, even with a layer of fabric and several feet of space separating us? I've never seen anything like *that*, the outline clear even through his suit pants.

I shift uncomfortably for hours, trying to ignore the nagging ache in my core, but there's no way I can sit that offers any relief. Every time I try to focus on something else, my mind's eye offers it up again, just like that.

I wonder what it would feel like, I think. *Maybe when you give him these documents, he'll shut his office door and bend you over his desk, pull down your panties and—*

I clear my throat and shake my head at my computer monitor.

Stop it, I tell myself. *You cannot fantasize about your boss. One, he's your boss. Two, he's your boss, and that's completely ridiculous.*

I'm sure he's got a girlfriend already.

There's no way he's interested in you — he's at least ten years older, and for the love of God, you're just his assistant.

I exhale and start typing again, but the ache doesn't go away.

I HAVE the documents on his desk by noon, but Kade isn't even in his office when I go to leave them. I'm half disappointed — despite myself, I'll take any chance to drown in the blue pools of his eyes, any chance to watch his chiseled jaw or check out the way his biceps strain against his shirt sleeves — and half glad that I can't make a fool of myself.

I need to go on a date, I think to myself.

I just need to get laid already. Get the big one over with, I'm sure then I'll think about my incredibly sexy bosses a little less...

"Jenna!" a female voice says behind me as I get back to myself. "Oh, my gosh, I'm so glad someone's not out at lunch. Got a minute?"

I turn and there's Blair. She's perky and blonde, the assistant to another of the law firm's partners, her blue eyes wide.

"Sure," I say.

"Larry's got this big luncheon meeting, and the sandwich delivery guy just dumped all his sandwiches at the reception desk and took off," she says, jerking one thumb over her shoulder and rolling her eyes in exasperation. "Usually they'll at least bring it in a little more and carry all the bags and stuff to the kitchen, you know? And I don't want the lunch to be late so I could really use a hand setting it all up if you don't mind..."

"No problem!" I say, probably a little *too* eagerly. I'm new here, after all, and I want to be good at my job. I want to be the employee who goes the extra mile, who tries a little extra hard.

You know, the employee who gets a raise and a promotion.

We grab all the sandwiches from the front desk and take them to the kitchen, where Blair arranges them onto a couple of platters while I fill some large glass pitchers with ice water.

"Thank you *so* much," Blair is saying as we walk down the hall, from the kitchen to the conference room. "This makes it so much easier, plus I feel like it's really unprofessional when I have to make a bunch of trips from the kitchen to the conference room?"

I frown. I have no idea why that might be unprofessional, but I make a mental note anyway.

"Of course," I say, just as she's about to push the door open. "Happy to—"

Blair walks through the door and holds it open with one elbow, both her hands holding sandwich platters.

Just as everyone in the room — several partners, plus their incredibly wealthy clients — looks up, her elbow slips and the door swings right into me and the two pitchers of water I'm carrying.

Everything feels like it's in slow motion as they slosh right into me, splashing freezing cold water over the front of my white shirt.

I feel like it happens in slow motion, because even before it does, I know *exactly* what the result will be. I know what happens when you get a white shirt wet.

And in a moment of horror, I remember my getting-ready frenzy that morning: the skirt I don't like, the shirt that doesn't quite fit me well.

And the garish, leopard print bra that I happen to be wearing. If it wasn't already half-visible through my shirt, now it is for *sure*.

I feel my face turn tomato-red, because everyone in the conference room is currently looking at me.

Including Kade and Lawson. I go redder, if that's even possible, and I freeze in the doorway, cold water dripping off me and onto the floor.

There's a moment of silence where no one seems to know what to say. Possibly because I'm telling almost all the partners of Hamilton, Clark, and Leonard, Attorneys at Law, what my undergarment preferences are.

"Oh!" Blair finally says, rushing to set the platters of sandwiches on the sideboard. "Oh, my gosh, let me get those from you, Jenna, go dry yourself off and I'll call the janitor for a mop…"

Right. Thank God *someone* is on top of her shit right now, because all I can think is *leopard print bra in front of your bosses.*

"Thanks," I manage to say, sounding halfway like a regular person. "I'll just, uh, go dry off…"

I turn quickly, trying to hide my humiliation and get out of the conference room as fast as I can. Most of the lawyers have already turned back to what they were doing, politely ignoring the drenched assistant in the doorway, but before I can get out of there I see two sets of eyes, still watching me.

Lawson.

Kade.

Even though my bosses look as different as can be, they've got a matching look in their eyes, a look I can't quite identify.

It's… dark. Serious. *Hungry.* I feel like I'm pinned to the wall by it, and despite the cold water on my front, I can feel my core heat up for a split second.

Then I rush out of the room and make a beeline for the restroom and paper towels.

CHAPTER FIVE

LAWSON

JENNA TURNS, RUSHING DOWN THE HALLWAY IN HER BLACK PUMPS. I watch her through the conference room's glass wall, blatantly staring at the sinful way her ass moves in that skirt, the curl of her strawberry-blonde hair against her neck as she rushes for the bathroom.

Hot pink leopard print.

Interesting.

No, it's more than interesting. Just like everything else about my assistant, it's fucking *irresistible*, the hint that below her sweet, good-girl demeanor there's something naughtier.

I wouldn't have pegged Jenna to be the kind of girl who'd wear lingerie like that to the office, but I like that she is.

Maybe she's naughty in other ways, too.

Near the end of the hallway, she turns right and pushes open the bathroom door, disappearing through it. I glance across the table at Kade, who just barely lifts one eyebrow as he meets my gaze.

He saw the same thing I just did, and now I know he's thinking the exact same thing.

I wait five minutes, and then I can't wait anymore. I nod at

Helen, the woman talking, and get up from the table, straightening my suit jacket and tie as I do, then walking through the door. Nonchalantly, I head down the hall and into the men's bathroom, pushing the door open silently and leaning against the wall.

"I didn't have you pegged as the flashy type," I say, letting my voice drop down to dangerous levels.

Jenna whirls around, her heels making a soft scraping noise on the shiny tiles of the bathroom.

The *men's* bathroom, where she's standing at the sinks with her shirt off, hot pink bra on full display.

"Lawson! I — uh — Mr. Marshall, what are you *doing*?" she yelps, instantly hugging her shirt to her chest, along with several handfuls of paper towels.

"Standing in the men's bathroom," I say, smirking at her.

The shirt and towels aren't hiding much. I can still make out the sinfully tempting curves of her body, the up-and-down swell of her chest as she breathes, her cleavage rising with every breath.

I can barely think. My mouth goes dry with desire and all I can think about is pressing my lips to her neck, my hands on her round, firm ass, the tiny gasp that would rise from her lips.

I could back her against the sinks in here, get that ugly bra off, make her moan as I rolled her nipples between my fingers, my leg between hers as I push her thighs apart...

"Men's?" she echoes, suddenly uncertain, wobbling just a little on her high heels.

I raise one eyebrow.

"Did you miss the urinals?" I ask, pointing into a corner.

She looks over at them, and to be fair, they're in an odd place — easy to miss if you're running in in a panic. Her cheeks color brightly the instant she sees them, her mouth opening in a surprised little O.

"I didn't— I thought this was—" she stammers.

The flush spreads from her cheeks down her neck and Jenna bites her lip, glancing from me to the urinals and back.

"They don't *typically* appear in the women's, or so I'm told," I tease her.

She smiles, just a little.

"I was in a rush," she says. "I was more worried about having a suddenly transparent shirt in front of everyone and I picked the wrong door..."

I take a step forward, like she's got a line hooked into me and she's pulling me forward. My attraction to this girl is magnetic, irresistible. I glance down at her chest one more time, because I swear I can feel the heat of her body from here.

"I promise not to tell if you don't," I say, letting my voice drop to a growl.

"Why would I tell?" she breathes, her eyes flicking up to my face. "I'm the one who fucked up, after all."

"Some mistakes are good ones," I tell her, taking another step closer.

My hands are still in my pockets, but being in the same room as Jenna half-naked — even though she's wearing a bra and has paper towels clutched to her chest — is going straight to my cock in the form of a massive erection.

Once more, her eyes flick downward. I *know* she sees it, just from the way her breath hitches in her throat.

"I should put my shirt back on and leave," she whispers. "I'm sorry for—"

The door swings open, and Jenna gasps as Kade walks in.

Just inside the door he stops and looks over at us, his dark eyes glowing from within. I've seen that look on his face before, even though it hasn't made an appearance in a long time.

The last time I saw it, we were in the VIP section of an exclusive club in Midtown, and a girl named Sapphire was straddling both our laps at once, her short skirt already riding up to her waist, thong exposed.

I'm sure Sapphire wasn't her real name, but we didn't give ours either. That's why condoms exist.

"You know this is the men's, don't you?" Kade growls, standing just inside the door.

Jenna sighs, still blushing.

"I do now," she says, shifting her weight in her high heels. "Look, I should put my clothes back on and get out—"

Kade flips the lock on the door.

"Closed for cleaning," he murmurs, his deep voice low.

CHAPTER SIX

KADE

Jenna's eyes widen even further, a flush creeping up her neck.

Lawson shoots me a look — no, a *glare* — that could probably cut through steel, but I meet his gaze steadily with an icy cool one of my own.

It's risky. I know this is risky. If I've read this situation wrong, any moment now Jenna could scream, and we'd both be out of jobs by the close of business today.

But I can't help myself. I believe in taking chances and, more importantly, seizing the moment.

And in this moment, I'm powerless to do anything but lock the door and watch Jenna, the swell in my chest *and* my pants quickly growing.

She nibbles on her lip for a moment, her wide eyes regarding me. She's nervous, sure, but she's not *afraid*.

"You don't look like the janitor," she finally says, a slight smile coming to her lips.

"You did have a spill, if I'm not mistaken," Lawson points out.

Jenna swallows, but she stands up straighter. The armful of paper towels that she's got clutched to her chest slips down slightly, revealing the twin swells of her breasts, the top of the ugly magenta bra. She doesn't bother fixing the towels.

"It was only water," she points out, tilting her head slightly to one side. "I'm not sure it needs two of the firm's top lawyers to help clean up."

Dear God, she's *flirting* with us.

Instantly, my cock is even harder, straining so hard against the zipper of my slacks that I'm afraid it'll burst them open. I don't look over at Lawson — I can't take my eyes off our assistant — but I'm certain that he's having the same problem right now.

A low, quiet growl erupts from deep within my chest, a noise I can't mask or contain. Luckily I don't think Jenna notices.

"Jenna," I start, my voice still gruff. "We're not here to—"

Lawson puts out his hand, cutting me off, and I let him, swallowing the rest of my sentence: *we're not here to dry you off, we're here to get you wet.*

He's right. He's always been the smooth, charming one between the two of us.

"We take our employees' issues *very* seriously," he says, voice low and dark. "And not only did you get yourself *very* wet, getting so wet seems to have impeded your ability to read bathroom signs."

She glances down, a tiny, embarrassed smile on her lips. Lawson takes another step toward her, and I exhale. I can't tear my eyes from the girl, from the way she's standing there, curves perfectly filling out her pencil skirt, her chest rising and falling with each breath.

My cock aches with the thought of what might come next: pressing myself to her back, her pale neck under my lips, pressing my cock between the perfect twin globes of her ass as Lawson kisses her ferociously, both of us making her moan at once.

My face between her thighs, spreading her legs as she leans

over the counter, gasping in pleasure as my tongue traces her slick folds...

"That's very kind of you," she demurs. "If you're worried about my ability to do my job, I assure you the lapse in my mental faculties was temporary. In fact, I'm already much better."

Her eyes flick over to me, and I see her take in the length of my tall, muscled body with a single glance. She doesn't linger over my tented slacks, but I know she sees it.

There's no way she *doesn't* see it.

Then Jenna takes a quick breath in, tightening her hands on the paper towels she's still holding to her chest.

And tosses them away, toward the garbage can.

"See?" she says, her eyes wide, her voice almost a whisper. "I'm dry already."

I can't stop myself any more. I step forward, walk behind her, rest my hands lightly on her bare shoulders.

I'm trembling with lust, my whole body tense like a spring at being so close to this forbidden girl who's consumed my every waking moment — and plenty of my sleeping ones — since she started here a few weeks ago.

I hear Jenna sigh, her body relaxing, and she sways back into me. Now we're touching nearly head-to-toe, my body taut and electrified.

I lean down, put my lips to her ear from behind. I swear I can feel her shiver slightly, and Lawson steps forward as well, slides a hand around her waist.

"Are you sure you're not wet at all?" I growl into her ear.

I slide my hands down her bare back, past the band of her bra, to skim over her hips. As much as I want to tear her clothes off right here, right now, I'm forcing myself to take it slowly. Think before acting.

Jenna's breath catches in her throat, and I put my lips on the spot right beneath her ear just as Lawson claims her mouth with his own.

CHAPTER SEVEN

JENNA

OH MY GOD.

Oh my GOD, what am I doing?!

Lawson kisses me hard, needy and rough enough to feel like his lips are bruising mine.

Needy and rough enough for me to forget myself completely, opening my lips under his and letting his tongue plunder into my mouth, taking whatever he wants from me.

At the same time, Kade plants his lips on my neck, the echoes of what he just said to me zinging back and forth through my brain.

Are you sure you're not wet at all?

His hands move across my hips, down the sides of my thighs. He's surprisingly gentle for someone so gruff, with such a reputation among the other secretaries for being ruthless in the courtroom and even with his colleagues.

And most of all, he's right. I'm dripping wet with need and desire, certain my panties are already soaked through even though I've only been standing in this bathroom for a few minutes.

With my *bosses.*

For a second, my brain screams in alarm — *you can't do this, it's against the rules, what if someone finds you here* — but then Lawson's fingers slip beneath my bra straps, pulling them down over my shoulders until one nipple is exposed to the cool air and I gasp, his mouth hovering over mine.

"I didn't have you pegged for the trashy lingerie type," he murmurs, his fingertips whispering over my nipple.

I moan quietly as it hardens under his touch at the same time Kade presses himself against my back, something thick and hard nestled between my buttocks.

That's his cock, a tiny voice in my head whispers. *It has to be, is it really that—*

Kade grabs my hips and pushes a little harder just as Lawson's fingers close around my nipple, rolling it lightly.

I moan again, louder this time.

"I don't usually wear this kind of thing," I manage to gasp out. "I meant to do laundry yesterday, but—"

"Don't apologize," Kade growls, his lips over the back of my neck. "There's nothing sexier than an innocent girl wearing something naughty."

His thumbs slip under the hem of my tight skirt, and slowly, he starts pushing it up my thighs.

I moan again, toes curling in my shoes. All at once I desperately want him to reach the top of my thighs, brush his fingers across my soaking panties and find out *just* how much I want this, but I'm also afraid of what might happen when he does.

I shouldn't want my bosses this much. It's *wrong*. I shouldn't be fantasizing about them every night when I go to sleep. I shouldn't be thinking wicked things about them as I ride the train to work every day.

More than anything I shouldn't be here, now, because what if—

Suddenly, there's a sharp knock on the door.

I freeze, gasping, my hand over my mouth.

Of *course* someone else wants to use the restroom. How could I be so stupid? I'm in a men's restroom in a place with a dozen male employees — of *course* someone else wants to use the bathroom!

I open my mouth to say something, maybe *I'm in here by accident, sorry, one minute*, but that wouldn't explain Lawson and Kade being in here, too.

But before I can say anything, Lawson puts his hand over my mouth with a wickedly charming smile.

"I'll be right out in a jiff," he calls, winking at me.

Despite everything, the wink still sets off butterflies in my stomach.

"What are you—" I whisper, but he cuts me off.

"Don't worry, peach," he murmurs back. "I've got this covered."

With that, Lawson gives me one more needy, bruising kiss, then turns and walks through the bathroom door, leaving me suddenly unsteady.

Kade's hands are still beneath the hem of my skirt, mid-thigh.

"We should go," I whisper nervously, but he just chuckles.

Then he suddenly spins me around until I'm facing him, wobbling just a little on my heels.

"Let Lawson do his thing," he growls, his voice sending shivers down my spine. "He's never let me down yet."

"I can't get caught," I whisper, searching his dark eyes for reassurance. "You can't get caught, I'm sure—"

"What did I just say?" he says, his voice low and teasing as one hand comes up to cup my chin, the pad of his thumb rough. "Don't worry, peach."

I swallow.

"Why are you calling me that?" I ask in a whisper.

Kade doesn't answer right away, but he slides his other hand over my ass, the motion so dangerous and possessive that I shudder with desire again.

28

What's wrong with me that I'm acting like this? I wonder.

"Because you're sweet, ripe, and juicy," he says, a twinkle his eye. "A shame I didn't get to find out how juicy, but that can wait for another day."

I blush again, hard, and Kade chuckles. He squeezes my ass with his other hand, his fingers right at the crevice between my thighs, and I can't help but arch my back a little.

I *want* those fingers on me, touching me *there*. I want him to find out how crazily, impossibly wet I am right now at the thought of both him *and* Lawson taking turns on me — or more.

"I shouldn't be doing this at all," I whisper, but I don't make a move to leave.

He just smirks, lowering his face to mine.

"I disagree, peach," he says.

Then he kisses me.

I'm surprised that Kade's kiss is gentler than Lawson's — I'd have bet anything that it would be the other way around. He kisses me slowly and surely, his tongue nudging between my lips until I part them for him, opening my mouth to him with a soft moan that I can't help.

He strokes my cheek as he kisses me, his other hand still in the cleft between my legs, making my desire pulse and pound, the need for them shaking me to my core. When he pulls back he's still smirking, then gently hands me my shirt from where I'd abandoned it on the bathroom sink.

"This should be almost dry," he says, letting his smooth voice bottom out. "And even if it's not, it wasn't as see-through as you think."

I take my shirt quickly, swallowing my nerves, and put it on. Kade watches me hungrily as I do all the buttons, then tuck it into my skirt and look at myself quickly in the mirror.

He's right. It's not really very see-through anymore, and in another ten minutes it'll be like nothing happened.

I bite my lip, taking a moment to smooth my hands over my outfit, Kade looking over my shoulder.

I don't *look* like someone who's fantasized about her bosses nonstop for weeks.

And I don't *look* like someone who just made out with them both, at the same time, in the company bathroom.

I can't do this again, a voice in my head whispers.

Are you sure? Another voice whispers back.

"I think you're safe to leave," Kade murmurs, his eyes locked with mine in the mirror. "I'm sure Lawson's taken care of whoever was out there."

"Taken care of...?" I ask, scenes from action movies dancing through my head, but Kade just chuckles.

"Talked them into using a different bathroom," he teases.

Then he squeezes my ass again and nudges me toward the door. Obediently, I walk, my heels clicking on the floor.

When I get there, I hold my breath. Kade is still watching me, his eyes devouring my image hungrily, his hands in his pockets as he leans against the sinks.

I grab the door. I unlock it, praying that no one is outside, that no one's about to watch me leave the men's bathroom while my boss stands behind me, looking like the cat that ate the canary.

Then, before I can think any more, I pull it open and walk through.

And sigh with relief.

The hallway is deserted. Not even Lawson is out here.

Head down, I walk back to my desk as quickly as I can.

No one seems to notice a thing.

CHAPTER EIGHT

LAWSON

It's easy to convince someone not to use a bathroom. Just tell them that there's been a vaguely-worded *mishap*, and they'll run away faster than you can say *monkey's uncle*.

Once I chase away the associate attorney who had to pee, I look at the bathroom door for another long moment. Every cell, every molecule in my body wants to go back in there and put my lips on Jenna's again, hear the way she sighs with pleasure as we both touch her in ways that *no one* should be touching an assistant.

I take a step toward the door. I'm imagining Kade in there, still, with her.

Even though we had an unspoken agreement — we *share* her — I'm still jealous.

I can't stop myself from imagining what could be going on. Is he kissing her, hiking her skirt over her waist? Does he have her bra off, tossed onto the floor as he hoists her onto the counter, one nipple already between his teeth?

Is my sweet peach whimpering with pleasure as he strokes his fingers along the edges of her wetness, feeling her excitement, her *desire* — all without me?

My hands clench into fists, desire pounding through my veins.

Go back in, it whispers. *Go in there, wrap her legs around you, give her what she so obviously wants.*

I take a deep breath and let it out.

I can't. We already almost got caught once, and that *can't* happen. We would all get fired, but worse, our reputations as attorneys would take a hit — we could get other jobs, of course. It wouldn't even be hard, but it wouldn't be somewhere as good as Hamilton, Clark, and Leonard.

No. I want it all — my job *and* the girl, so I turn on my heel and walk away, back down the hallway to my office.

There, I read through tedious memos and pages and pages of court transcripts until I'm no longer imagining Jenna, face flushed, lying back on my desk while we fuck her.

AT FIVE-FIFTEEN THAT AFTERNOON, Paul Leonard raps on the jamb on my office door and then steps inside, unannounced.

I look up at him, a quick bolt of panic shooting through my chest. Leonard is the oldest, most senior partner at the firm. He's basically retired by now — he spends far more time on the golf course than he does in the office — but he's still the big boss, at the top of the food chain.

And there's no reason for him to be stopping by my office, unannounced, himself. Why wouldn't he send his assistant?

"Paul," I say smoothly, standing from my desk chair and buttoning my jacket. "To what do I owe the honor?"

A moment later, Jenna appears behind him, wide-eyed and startled. She's supposed to announce any and all visitors to Kade and me, but I've no doubt that Paul Leonard simply strode past her with a single nod, and Jenna's not about to stop *him*.

"Mr. Leonard is here to see you?" she says, her voice nervous, her eyes flicking to him.

I can't help but smile. Even like this, nervous as a rabbit, she's gorgeous. Irresistible. Completely—

Not now, Lawson, I tell myself.

"Thank you, Jenna," I say.

She holds my gaze for just a moment too long, and even though the man standing between us holds my job in his hands, I can't help the bolt of desire that courses through me. It's visceral, tangible, almost unreal how much I want this girl.

"Go home," I tell her. "I'll see you in the morning."

Even though I'd rather see you tonight, after hours.

She ducks her head and steps out of my view, while Paul Leonard comes in and sits in one of the leather chairs positioned in front of my desk. Even though he's in my office, he waves his hand at me to sit as well, and I do.

"The DiMaggio trademark case," he says without preamble.

"Kade and I are still working discovery on that, along with—"

He waves his hand again, dismissively this time.

"Not my concern at the moment," he says. "I'm sure the two of you are building something that'll utterly destroy these Trentine assholes in court, you always do. No. I'm here because the President and CFO of DiMaggio Holdings wants to meet the attorneys working on their case."

I lean back in my office chair, waiting for him to continue.

"Tomorrow," he says.

"Of cour—"

"In London," he goes on. "He's flying the two of you out for four days. First class. Along with Miss McAlister, so you've got someone to take notes."

He shrugs.

London? Shit.

"Don't know why he insists on flying her out as well. These

days, can't your phone take notes for you in meetings? The things can practically wipe your ass!" he says, then slaps his knee.

I smile because he's my boss, not because it was funny.

"It's his money," I say levelly.

"Damn right it is, so he wants you in the UK for a few days of meeting and whatever it is he's got for you to do," he says, then pushes his hands against his knees and levers himself to standing, adjusting his jacket as he does.

"If your girl's already gone you can have mine book you the tickets, though you'd probably better tell her what her weekend plans are," he says, the words trailing over his shoulder, Paul Leonard already halfway out the door.

I tilt my head back against my expensive leather desk chair and exhale hard, because I've got a mountain of work on my plate already and don't need four days of travel to compound it.

Jenna's coming with us, I think.

It'll be just the three of us.

No one else from the firm. No nosy secretaries, no glowering boss.

Just us, in a hotel. For four days.

Alone in my office, I grin widely at nothing at all.

CHAPTER NINE

KADE

London?

Paul Leonard has to be fucking kidding me.

As he walks back through my office door, I fight the urge to throw a stapler at the back of his head, because he thinks he can just up and tell me that tomorrow, I'm going to another country.

The shitty part is that he's right. He *can* tell me that, because a client demands it and this is America, where the customer is always right.

Even though I've got piles and piles of work to get through, most of it for his case. Even though I had plans this weekend that didn't involve being on a plane for nine hours.

Plus, that's four days that I won't see our peach, Jenna. Four days that I'll be jerking off in a hotel room, halfway across the globe, thinking about how soft her thighs were beneath my fingers and how badly I want to do *so* much more to her.

I've no sooner stood from my desk, figuring I'll go talk to his secretary about travel plans in person, then Lawson is there, standing in my doorway, arms crossed as he leans against the jamb.

"You excited for our little trip?" he says, an unmistakable twinkle in his eye.

I stand. I glower.

What the hell is he so happy about?

"Not particularly," I say, crossing my arms over my chest.

Is he being sarcastic?

Lawson lifts one eyebrow.

"Leonard didn't mention it to you," he says, matter-of-factly.

I sigh, because I'm getting the feeling that Lawson is toying with me right now, and it's the last thing I need.

"Didn't mention what?" I snap. "That he wants us to put everything aside and fly across the world tomorrow at his whim, and we're going to do it because he's paying us *gobs* of money? Yes, Law, he did mention that part."

"No," he says, and now he's grinning.

It's a fucking irritating grin.

"He wants us to bring Jenna."

There's a brief moment of silence, and then the blood roars through my ears so loudly that for a moment, I can't hear anything else.

Then it recedes, only to be transported directly to my dick.

Four days.

In another city.

With Jenna.

"He does?" I say, my mouth slow to catch up with my brain. "What for?"

"Someone to take notes, he says."

Lawson steps forward, crosses my office toward me, and puts both hands on my desk, leaning in slightly.

"That's three nights in a hotel room," he murmurs.

I know *exactly* what he's thinking.

"Three nights with no one else from the firm," I continue. "Three nights where no one can cost us our jobs."

Now Lawson's grinning again, and it makes him look almost

feral. I'm sure I must have the same look in my eyes, a glimmer of hope and lust.

Three nights that we can spend with our sweet peach Jenna. Three nights to claim her, feel her velvet skin against ours, make her sigh and moan.

Three nights to make her come so hard and so many times that she loses count, three nights to share her with my best friend while we give her the best time of her life.

I'm already getting hard, just thinking about a hotel room.

It's fucking ridiculous.

"Good," I bark out, more harshly than I mean to.

Lawson just laughs.

AT LEAST THEY got us first-class tickets, because first-class on an international flight ain't half bad.

On this one, each first-class seat reclines fully, contained within its own short-walled pod. There's a TV opposite the chair, a desk tray that pulls out, and endless wine. For an airplane, it's spacious and luxurious.

I get the seat-pod by the window, while Lawson and Jenna sit across the aisle, in the middle of the plane, Jenna on the side nearer to me.

I watch her as she sits down, stuffing her gear away. It's obvious that she's never flown first class before from the way she looks around the cabin in wonder, and from the way she asks the flight attendant how much the champagne costs.

It's free, of course. We're in first class.

Lawson sits in the seat-pod adjoining Jenna's, but since there's a plastic divider between them I'm not jealous.

Until he slides the divider down. Then I'm a *little* jealous.

I'm more jealous as he winks at her, sinking back in his seat as it reclines, smiling his nice, easy smile. I can see her relax from here, as the free champagne and Lawson work their magic.

Not yet, I remind myself. *You're on a plane. There's a grandma with a hearing aid two feet behind you and a family with two small kids a row up. I think the woman in 3B is probably a nun.*

It doesn't help. I'm already imagining myself kneeling in front of Jenna's seat as I pull away her leggings, inhaling her scent. Burying my face in the sweet wetness between her legs, feeling her stiffen and relax underneath my hands as I lap her slowly but steadily, making her wait for her first orgasm.

"Can I get you anything else?" the flight attendant asks with a charming British accent, plucking the empty champagne glass from my hand as I feast my eyes on Jenna, my thoughts only on her.

I glance up at the woman. Cute, but no competition. I shouldn't have another drink, because I've got ten hours of work to do on a nine-hour flight, but my eyes are glued to Jenna and Lawson and it's taking everything I've got not to leap over the aisle, claim her mouth with mine.

"Wine," I say, more gruffly than I mean to. "Red wine."

The flight attendant smiles like I didn't just bark a command at her.

"Right away, sir," she says, and gracefully walks down the aisle.

I lean back in my chair. Lawson glances over, looking perfectly at home and relaxed.

He's still talking to Jenna, his hand on her side of the divider.

I'm not jealous. *I'm not jealous.*

I'm just going to need that wine.

CHAPTER TEN

JENNA

I'VE NEVER FLOWN FIRST CLASS BEFORE. I DON'T THINK I'VE EVER flown business class before.

Hell, the fanciest I've ever flown was the time that I traded places with someone who wanted to sit next to his girlfriend and I got the exit row. That was *nice*.

But it's nothing compared to this — my own personal pod, on an airplane. Free champagne, free drinks, with a seat that reclines into a bed and my own larger-than-usual TV screen.

It sure beats the hell out of trying to fall asleep with a blown up pillow around my neck while the guy next to me in economy snores like a dying rhinoceros.

I lift the last bite of my brownie to my lips, then wipe my fingers on the napkin. A cloth napkin. The silverware is real metal, not the plastic stuff you get in economy.

"How was it?" Lawson asks from a few feet away.

My heart hammers, even though the question is totally innocuous. For a few hours now, as we ate and drank, we've just been chatting. Kade, sitting across the aisle from me, chimes in every now and again.

It's... *pleasant*. Right now Lawson doesn't feel like my boss. I don't feel like his employee.

I feel like we're flirting, but that's only because we are. We shouldn't be — even if we don't know anyone else on this plane, we shouldn't be — but we are.

Kade, too, watching from across the aisle with his dark eyes glimmering, teasing, almost *taunting* me.

I haven't forgotten what happened in the bathroom yesterday. There's no *way* I could forget it, so every interaction we have is laced with the weight of tension, with the memory of Kade asking me how wet I was with his lips on my ear.

"It was great," I answer honestly. Maybe not bakery-great, but for airplane food?

Divine.

"You're not going to get a taste for the good life now, are you?" Lawson teases me. "You'll be demanding a raise from us in no time."

Across the aisle, Kade flips his desk tray away, stands, and stretches. It's the first time I've seen either of them in anything but a suit — Kade in jeans that fit him *perfectly* and a t-shirt that shows off every ripple of his perfectly muscled body, Lawson in sweatpants that somehow make his ass look amazing and a shirt that I already want to tear off his body.

"Next thing we know she'll be ordering Dom Perignon for lunch meetings," he says, his low voice crackling through the air, shivering down my skin.

I bite my lip, starting to get warm despite myself.

You're on a plane with hundreds of other people, I remind myself. *Some of them are two feet away. Nothing is going to happen here.*

"She'll be walking in wearing designer heels and demanding to know who ate the leftover Kobe steak she left in the fridge," Lawson teases.

I blush, my stomach knotting, my core starting to overheat.

"If I were eating Kobe steak, I bet I'd go out for lunch, not bring in leftovers," I tease right back.

Lawson grins. Above me, Kade chuckles.

"See? She's already got ideas," Kade says. "She'll have to fly economy on the way back."

"Oh, come on," I mock-protest. "I'd have to report you to the ethics committee or something."

They both go instantly still, just for a moment. My mouth is suddenly dry, and I grab the glass of red wine I got with dinner — in a *real* wine glass — and down it.

"Kidding," I say quietly.

But the spell is broken. Lawson leans forward in his chair, toward me, toward the gap in the barrier between us.

"You know this is dangerous, don't you, peach?" he murmurs.

Instantly, my skins fizzes like someone's poured sparkling water on it, and I gulp.

"Yes," I whisper.

He moves forward in his chair, leaning toward me and his fingers find my knee. I'm covered in an airplane blanket already, because airplanes are always *freezing*, but I shiver with desire at his touch.

"And you know we're going to do this anyway, don't you?" Kade rumbles above me. He's still standing there casually, one arm slung atop the short plastic wall surrounding my first-class pod, but his eyes are dark and dangerous, promises held within.

Just as I'm trying to figure out what to say, the lights go out.

I gasp and blink, startled, but Lawson just chuckles again. The running lights along the two aisles are still lit, and none of the other passengers seem alarmed.

"That just means it's bedtime," Lawson purrs.

"Yeah, when the flight crew wants us all to shut up and go to sleep," Kade says above me. "Bother them a little less."

"Well—" I start, but I'm startled by Lawson's hand slipping under the cheap fleece blanket.

I lock eyes with him, and he smiles wickedly.

"You interested in sleeping, peach?" he whispers, fingers moving up my thigh.

My heart's thudding in my chest and I bite my lip again, trying not to betray my nervousness as his hand moves ever upward, stealthy beneath the blanket.

I can't believe this is happening. I can't believe this—

Casually, Lawson reaches behind himself and slides the door to his pod shut, closing us off from the airplane's other aisle. Kade is still standing on my other side, blocking my door, and suddenly what seemed so public a moment ago is incredibly intimate.

Someone behind me snorts and coughs.

Well, kind of intimate.

Lawson's fingers move again, further up my thigh, and I swallow hard as I move my knees apart on the airplane seat, leaning back slightly, inviting him in despite myself. Despite *knowing* better than this, I grip the armrests as tightly as I can and roll my hips toward him, trying not to make any noise.

On top of the plastic wall, Kade's hand closes into a fist, and with heavy-lidded eyes I glance down at the zipper on his jeans. It's tented outward, a clearly *massive* erection straining at the material.

"Like what you see?" Lawson asks, his voice low and rough.

Before I can answer, his fingers reach the top of my thighs, stroking along the inside, and his hand brushes my hip through the thin material of my leggings.

A tiny gasp escapes my lips, and I clamp my mouth shut instantly, terrified of making noise.

"Shh," Lawson teases. "No reason for you to make a scene."

"Not that they could throw us out," Kade points out.

Still leaning against the wall, with his other hand, he slowly cups himself, fingers pressing into the denim of his pants, making the outline of his thick cock clear as day.

My eyes go even wider, and at the same time, Lawson runs his fingers over my lower lips and clit, the friction of the fabric between us zipping deliciously through my body.

Now I'm panting for breath, writhing in my airplane seat. I can't tear my eyes away from Kade's cock, magnificent even through a layer of denim, and I know that Lawson's grinning at me hungrily, his fingers now seeking the waistband of these leggings.

What are you doing? A tiny voice in my head asks weakly. *You know this is a bad idea, you could get caught...*

I banish the voice as his hand finds the elastic around my waist and instantly dives below it, moving past my mound and into my slick wetness.

I sigh, eyes rolling back into my head at the feel of his hand on me at last, his skilled fingers sliding between my lips, sampling me.

"Oh..." I whisper, then clench my teeth shut again.

Lawson pushes one finger inside me, just to the first knuckle, and I arch my back and move my hips off the chair, toward him.

I want more. I *need* more, but instead he stops suddenly.

I open my eyes, and he's looking at me in surprise.

"Peach," he murmurs, his voice so low only Kade and I can hear it. "Are you a virgin?"

My heart bangs against my ribcage again, and in the sudden silence, I'm convinced that everyone can hear it as I gather my nerve.

You should lie, I think. *Don't tell them you've never had sex before, there's no way they'll want to keep going...*

"Yes," I say. "But don't stop, please..."

Lawson grins again, and above me, Kade's gravelly voice chuckles.

"Not for the world," he murmurs.

"We're going to be your first," Lawson says, drawing even

43

closer to me in the confines of the airplane seats. "That thought is so fucking sexy, peach. I can barely stand it."

His fingers slide further into me. My knees are as wide as they can go, and as my eyelids flutter, my gaze falls on Kade's cock again. I can't help but imagine *that* inside me, even though it seems impossible.

"Both of you?" I ask, my voice a ragged whisper.

Lawson's fingers move inside me, and suddenly he hits a spot that makes my vision go white and my whole body jolt with pleasure. I moan quietly, then instantly clap one hand over my mouth, eyes opening wide in surprise.

"Shh," Lawson teases.

"Wouldn't want anyone knowing what you're up to," Kade says, a smirk in his voice.

Lawson's fingers keep moving, stroking the sweet spot inside me and driving me insane. I clench my teeth behind my hand, forcing myself not to moan, eyelids fluttering as I look at Kade.

His eyes are heavy-lidded with lust, and every time my hips jolt and roll he breathes a little harder, watching his best friend finger me.

It's insane. It's dangerous.

I couldn't stop even if I wanted to, which I don't. I want to keep doing this and more forever.

Lawson moves forward, pulls his fingers out of me and in one quick motion, pulls my leggings and thong down to my knees. I'm still covered by the airplane blanket, but now my wetness is against the warm leather beneath me, the slight rumble of the plane coming through the seat.

"Get those off," Lawson whispers.

I glance over at Kade, nervous again. What if something happens and we have to get off the plane?

"Peach," Lawson growls, and with one look at the promise in his eyes, I kick my leggings the rest of the way off. If we have a water landing, I'll just have to go down that slide half-naked.

"Good girl," Kade groans above me, Lawson's hand snaking back up under the blanket. He's still patient, still gentle, but there's an urgency in his movements that wasn't there before.

Kade touches himself again, his heavy-lidded eyes watching mine, the outline of his massive erection still incredibly obvious through his jeans.

I take a deep breath, arching in my seat, my legs as wide as they'll go in the confined space. British Airways is going to have to throw this blanket away and possibly replace the seat, but this feels *so* good that I can't even think about stopping.

Lawson's fingers reach my clit, circling the delicate nub, sliding through my wetness. I whimper, one fist to my mouth, the other desperately clutching the arm rest as Kade strokes himself through his jeans again, Lawson's fingers doing delicious things to me.

Kade's fingers rise to his zipper. They pinch it. I can barely breathe as he lowers it slowly, without a single thought that anyone else can see or that at any moment, a flight attendant could come by and ask what we're doing.

Lawson slides two fingers inside me, his thumb still slow and delicious on my clit as I pant with lust. The zipper on Kade's jeans reaches the bottom as Lawson's fingers start to move inside me, rocking me back and forth in the seat with ripples of pleasure.

Kade looks down at me, a lusty smirk on his face.

"Go on," he says.

I reach one hand out, barely able to think over the roar of lust in my brain, but my fingers seem to reach his open zipper all on their own, then slide inside. I grip his enormous hardness as Lawson brings me closer and closer to the edge and Kade groans quietly, from deep in his chest, at my touch.

I bite my lip, eyes half-fluttering closed, as I close my hand around Kade's shaft, and a moment later it springs free of his jeans and I gasp as he groans again, almost too loudly this time.

It's *huge*, long and thick, standing proudly at attention in the dim light, the head a red-purple and hard as a rock. I can barely fit my hand around it, and for a moment I just stare, until Kade looks down at me, wraps his hand around mine, and pumps it up and down his shaft.

A pearlescent drop gathers at the tip, and I can tell that Kade's doing everything in his power right now not to make any noise or alert the other first-class passengers to what we're doing, but I'm fascinated. I pump his cock again, feeling every muscle in his body tense, another drop joining the first at the tip.

Lawson's fingers move deeper, his thumb on my clit speeding up and sending a whirlwind of pleasure and desire shuddering through my body. I'm going to come soon, right here on this plane, unsuspecting passengers all around me.

But I can't help myself. Kade's massive erection still in my hand, I lean forward slightly and wrap my lips around the tip, eliciting a gasp from above.

Suddenly Lawson pushes a third finger into my tight channel, stretching me but moving his hand all at the same time, hitting that spot of pure pleasure right inside me as his thumb strokes my clit. I move my lips down Kade's shaft as I try not to whimper, a big hand suddenly on the back of my head.

"You look so fucking sexy right now, peach," he murmurs, his voice barely audible above the white noise of the airplane's cabin.

He fills my mouth completely and I take him in as far as I can, the tip of his cock bumping against the back of my mouth as I swirl my tongue around. I want to hear him groan like that again, want to show my boss as much pleasure as I possibly can.

"Come for us," Lawson murmurs on my other side, fingers moving even faster and deeper inside me. "We want to watch you come, peach."

I slurp back along Kade's cock, his hand now fisted in my hair as pleasure drives through me, my whole body shaking with the force of it. The airplane blanket has fallen off me already, my leggings around my ankles, but I don't care anymore.

I *want* them. I want *this*, and as I spiral closer and closer to coming, I moan into Kade's cock, my hand locked in a fist around the base.

I take him as deep as I can one more time, and then all at once I come as Lawson strokes *that* spot again, his fingers perfectly in time with his thumb. The wave of pleasure breaks over me, and despite everything, I moan my orgasm into Kade's cock, my whole body shuddering as Lawson's fingers keep working their magic.

His fist tightens in my hair and for a moment I can't move at all as another wave of pleasure washes through my body, and then his cock jolts in my mouth as I suck eagerly, swallowing every last drop, licking and sucking until he's got nothing left.

When I finally pull back I'm spent, almost delirious. Lawson pulls his fingers out of me as I collapse back into my airplane seat, panting for breath. As I watch, he puts them slowly into his mouth, one by one, licking my juices off.

I'm fascinated. Above me, Kade groans quietly, almost like he's jealous. I can't believe that he's doing this — it's dirty as hell but also unbelievably hot, all at once.

"Delicious," Lawson grins at me when he's finished. "I've wanted to taste you since the day you interviewed for your job, peach, and it's just as good as I imagined."

I have no idea what to say to that, so instead I just swallow and fumble with the blanket, pulling it back over my lap. I don't even bother pulling my leggings up yet — I feel totally spent, and getting pants back on isn't even something I can worry about right now.

"Next time it's my turn," Kade rumbles from above, tucking his cock back into his pants.

"You'll—" Lawson starts, but he's interrupted by a female voice from behind Kade.

"Is everything all right here?" a flight attendant asks, her voice low in the quiet cabin.

I jump nearly out of my seat with surprise, but Kade just calmly turns around and Lawson looks up from where he's sitting in his own seat, perfectly casual.

"Just lovely, thanks," Kade says, a smirk around his eyes.

CHAPTER ELEVEN

LAWSON

I SLEEP LIKE A BABY FOR THE REST OF THE FLIGHT, DREAMING OF the way Jenna looks when she comes, the feeling of her pussy clenching around me as she did.

Watching her suck Kade's cock. The way she *moaned* when she did, how greedily she sucked him down. I'm still hard as a rock as I drift off to sleep in my first-class seat, but I'm a grown man.

I know how to wait a little while for what I want.

When Jenna wakes up, about an hour before landing, there's a moment when she suddenly glances at me, like she's trying to remember whether what happened was a dream or real, glancing from my face to my fingers.

I grin at her, give the girl a wink. She blushes. Even though a few hours ago I was knuckle-deep inside her while she had my best friend's cock in her mouth, she blushes.

I lean forward, crook one finger at her. She leans forward, toward me.

"It all really happened," I whisper. "And just as soon as we get to the hotel, I'm going to taste your sweet pussy the old-fashioned way."

She swallows hard, pulling back a little, glancing around to see if anyone can hear.

They can't. I chuckle.

"And we won't be stopping until you're screaming our names, peach," I finish.

She looks over at Kade, who's scowling at the airplane TV in front of him, mashing the buttons on his armrest like there's nothing good on. He always has trouble sleeping on airplanes, so he's probably been awake most of this time, trying to find something to do.

He seems to sense her watching him, though, and meets her eyes for a long second, letting his gaze travel down her body. At last Jenna, blushing, breaks eye contact and starts shoving magazines back into the pocket in her seat.

Kade looks at me and grins.

∿

I'VE GOT plans for our arrival in London. The car will be at the airport to take us to the hotel, where we'll have a few hours to freshen up before our first meeting at 1pm.

The second we get into that hotel, Jenna is *ours*. I know we shouldn't have done that to her on the airplane like that, but I can't help myself around the girl — all rational thought flies right out the window with one look at her beautiful face, and I'm instantly lost.

But when we finally get through customs at Heathrow Airport, instead of the usual driver waiting for us, holding a sign with our last names, there are two men — one *clearly* not a driver.

"Welcome to London, Mr. Marshall, Mr. Chandler, Miss McAlister," he says, his voice formal. "I'm Niall, it's a pleasure to meet you in person. I believe we spoke on the phone?"

"Yes," Jenna pipes up, putting down her bag and holding out her hand. "Nice to meet you."

He clears his throat as he shakes her hand.

"I'm afraid that I'll be taking you directly from the airport to the offices," he says. "I understand that you'd probably like some time to freshen up, but Mr. Evanston has indicated that there have been some developments and he'll be needing to speak to you directly."

My heart sinks, along with my cock. I was half-hard just walking through the airport, thinking of the delicious things I was going to do to Jenna the moment we were alone again. I was aching to taste her in the back of the limousine, push her soft thighs apart as I lick her sweet pussy, her hips arching off the seat...

"Of course," Kade says next to me, his voice little more than a growl. "As long as George doesn't mind seeing us in our travel clothes, I didn't exactly wear a three-piece suit on the airplane."

Niall smiles, and he somehow looks very British while doing it.

"Naturally," he says, as the driver steps forward and begins loading our luggage onto a cart.

I exchange a glance with Kade, and I can tell that we're both wracking our brains right now, trying to come up with a reason that we need an hour at the hotel, or at least somewhere that we won't be supervised. I know my best friend and colleague well enough to know that he wants the exact same thing that I do — Jenna, moaning our names over and over again.

Jenna, coming hard, the beautiful pink flush in her cheeks as we bring our peach to ecstasy over and over again. I want to bury myself inside her sweet virgin pussy, make her beg for release when she can't take it anymore.

I want to share her with him. I want to watch her as she completely loses control to the feeling of *both* of us, completely in our power as she experiences more pleasure than she could possibly imagine.

But instead, as I follow Niall to the waiting car, I clench my fists and say nothing, because we *can't* be found out.

To my dismay, Niall also climbs into the back of the limousine with us, and the driver closes the door behind all four before pulling into the heavy airport traffic. Even though he's there, I can't take my eyes off her — even the way she pulls her strawberry-blonde hair back from her face has me watching her neck, wondering what kind of noises she'd make when I suck the soft skin there.

I look at Kade again. His mouth is a hard, straight line, and I know he's just as disappointed as I am.

"There have been some serious developments in the case, I'm afraid," Niall starts. "To begin, it turns out that the claim made by Trentine Industries seems to change by the hour…"

Jenna shifts slightly in her seat. I swallow hard, drink some of the water that Niall's offered us.

Soon, peach, I promise her silently.

CHAPTER TWELVE

KADE

Fuck DiMaggio holdings.

Fuck Trentine Industries.

Fuck everything and everyone standing between me and Jenna and Lawson right now, between her pretty pink lips around my cock while Lawson buries his face between her thighs.

Fuck everything between her in my hotel room shower, wet and naked, the water dripping down her body like sin as my mouth devours hers and Lawson takes her from behind, the lust quickly clouding over her eyes as I reach down between her legs and rub her clit while he—

"Any questions?" the man at the head of the table asks, and I snap back to reality, away from the thoughts I can't control.

Lawson and I glance at each other quickly. Just long enough for me to know that he hasn't been paying proper attention either. Luckily George, Niall's boss and a classic stuffy old British man, doesn't seem to notice as he takes off his reading glasses and wipes them.

"Can Trentine back up their claim that the mark was in use by them before DiMaggio's first products came out in nineteen sixty-two?" I ask, even though I've got a bad feeling that George has already answered it in his long-winded spiel.

George sighs. He laces his hands together in front of himself and looks at me, his chin wobbling.

"That's the crux of the case, isn't it? They claim it was, but their evidence is somewhat lacking. If we can show that it wasn't we'll have this wrapped up in a bow with a ribbon on top, but I'm afraid that it's going to be quite tricky," George says.

Lawson and I both nod. We've done a thousand trademark cases before — corporate intellectual property is our specialty, and it's one that's made us both very wealthy men — but this one is far more complicated than most, spanning fifty years and two continents.

"It shouldn't present a real stumbling block," Lawson says, his smile and charm instantly smoothing everything over. "Kade and I thrive on tricky, tough-to-crack cases, don't we?"

I swallow hard, forcing thoughts of my assistant bent over the bathroom counter out of my head.

"Of course," I say.

With that, George Evanston stands, snapping his folder closed. His assistant, a middle-aged woman with salt-and-pepper hair in a bun also stands, tucking her pen away in a briefcase.

Jenna clears her throat quickly, nervously tapping her pen on the pad in front of her. She hasn't said a word this whole time, though she's been writing furiously. Longhand — George is so afraid of corporate espionage that he won't allow anyone to take notes using a tablet or laptop.

"Excuse me," she says, her voice quiet and a little nervous.

Now we're all standing, and I force my eyes ahead, to George's balding head, instead of at my assistant's perfect ass in her tight leggings, since none of us has changed clothes since yesterday.

God, the things I would do to that ass. I can still practically *feel* the way those two perfect globes hugged my cock, even through my pants, and for just a split second I let my self-control go and I'm imagining her, astride me reverse-cowgirl, the tip of my cock just barely sliding through that tight back hole—

"Yes, Miss McAlister?" George asks, his London accent genteel but slightly impatient.

But our peach holds her ground.

"Can you remind me what date you wanted to move forward with discovery?" she asks.

"I'd like it by the end of next week," he says. "Is that all?"

Jenna leans forward slightly, writing that down on her notepad, and it takes everything I've got not to come up behind her and bend her over the rest of the way, grabbing her hair and pulling her head back while I suck at the tender skin on her neck.

Fuck. *Fuck*, I have to stop doing this.

"That's it," says Lawson smoothly, shooting me a glance as he does. He can probably tell that I'm barely listening, utterly lost in thought with my mind elsewhere. "We'll see you at the restaurant tonight, of course."

"Seven-thirty on the dot, and don't be late," George says, and then he tosses a scarf around his neck and walks from the conference room, followed by his assistant.

God*damn* it, I'd forgotten about the dinner tonight. Of course we've got a dinner with clients, at one of London's poshest restaurants, with all the top people at DiMaggio Holdings — the President, CEO, CFO, and several other people whose titles I don't even remember right now.

Meaning instead of easing Jenna onto my cock as she kneels over me tonight, panting for breath, her nipples between Lawson's fingers, I'm going to be eating steak, drinking vintage red wine, and desperately wishing to be back in my hotel room already.

"Bloody hell," I mutter to the almost-empty room, half-mocking our British client.

"You've got the accent all wrong," Lawson chides me, teasing.

"I wasn't trying for an accent," I say, not in the mood for his jokes. "I was trying to swear about tonight's dinner."

"What's wrong with Le Chevalier?" Jenna asks, innocent as anything.

Lawson and I look at each other. I'm still scowling, but there's a hint of amusement in his eye.

And then, as he looks around the room and seems to realize something, there's a hint of something far wickeder.

"There's nothing wrong with Le Chevalier, peach," he says, his voice lowering to a purr as he walks toward Jenna. I can practically see her pulse skyrocket as he does, her pupils dilating with sudden desire.

"Then..."

Lawson interrupts her without missing a beat, hoisting her onto the conference table and pushing her knees apart, running his hands up the insides of her thighs.

"There's something else I'd *much* rather be doing," he says.

My face breaks into a wolfish grin.

CHAPTER THIRTEEN

JENNA

TEN THOUSAND ALARM BELLS GO OFF IN MY HEAD AS LAWSON kisses me roughly, urgently, his hands already between my legs before I've even had a moment to think.

Instantly my body surrenders to him, my mouth opening beneath his, a small, urgent noise escaping my lips. This is all I've thought about since our encounter on the airplane — but we haven't had another moment alone.

Until now.

In this conference room.

Oh my God.

My eyes fly open and I pull back for just a moment, head swiveling as I look at our surroundings, but I didn't need to worry. Instead of a modern, glass-walled, light and airy conference room like the ones we've got back in New York, this one is thoroughly Old World — dark wood paneling, lined with bookshelves.

There's not a window anywhere.

Lawson moves his lips to my ear, nips at my earlobe, and chuckles softly.

"You think I didn't check that first thing, peach?" he asks, the growl in his voice sending shivers straight down my spine. "I'm not about to let anyone else see the things we're about to do to you, because you're *all* ours."

I swallow hard, desire blossoming within me. The conference table shakes slightly, and I look behind myself to see Kade on his knees behind me, fingers whispering down my neck.

I shiver again, my eyes stuttering closed for a moment.

Don't, I think to myself, desperately. *Go back to the hotel where there are doors that lock, anyone could walk in at any moment…*

"We shouldn't do this here," I murmur as Kade's fingers find their way up and into my hair. "Someone could walk in on —"

His fingers suddenly lock, pulling my head back toward him. He claims my mouth roughly and I give in completely as his tongue plunders my mouth, his grip never once letting up.

Finally, he pulls back a fraction of an inch, and at the same time Lawson's thumb sweeps over the spot between my legs and I gasp in pleasure, even though he's touching me through my leggings.

"What was that?" Kade murmurs, his voice dark and deep. "If you want us to stop, just say the word, peach."

My breath is coming in shallow gasps, and I try to force myself to form the words: *no, stop, let's just go back to the hotel where it's safe…*

But I can't. It's not what I *really* want, because what I *really* want is dirty beyond words, totally filthy.

I want both my bosses to take my virginity at the same time.

Right here.

Right now.

On this conference table.

"We're waiting," Lawson says, teasing me as his lips make their way down my neck and my eyes side closed again.

Kade slides his other hand down the neck of my shirt, my head still back, palming my breast and pinching one nipple between two fingers, making me sigh.

"Tell us to stop anytime you want, peach," Kade growls. "We'll give you *exactly* what you want."

I swallow, still panting. I lick my lips, eyes still closed, as I try to gather my wits.

"Don't stop," I finally manage to whisper over the roar of lust in my head.

They both chuckle quietly.

"We wouldn't dream of it," Lawson says, and before I know it his hands are at the waistband of my leggings and he pulls hard. For the second time in twenty-four hours I lift my hips to let him undress me, and in the blink of an eye my shoes and leggings are tossed somewhere else.

Instantly, his hands are cupping my ass, then sliding me to the edge of the table. I bite my lip hard so I don't yelp, but Lawson is already shoving my thighs apart with his rough hands, sucking at the soft, tender skin as he works his way up from my knee.

I'm reeling, still astonished at what's happening, leaning back on my hands as I watch Lawson's sandy head between my legs.

"What are you…" I start to ask, but I cut myself off, because it's perfectly obvious what he's doing.

But he answers me anyway.

"I'm going to lick your sweet pussy until you come for me," he answers, looking up with pure sin in his eyes. "God, you're so fucking wet for me right now."

I can't even answer. No one's *ever* talked to me that way before — not even close — but my God, I think I like it. It sends a spike of heat downward through my body like I've never felt.

Kade bends over me, his lips on my neck, both hands now down my shirt doing *incredible* things to my nipples.

"And when he's finished, I'm going to make you come again," he says, voice rough with need. "First I'm going to watch you come for me and then I'm going to have you myself, peach."

I open my mouth to answer him, but instead he captures it again, his tongue against mine before I can think, at the same time that Lawson's fingers brush my soaking wet lips, his breath hot on me.

I moan into Kade's mouth. I try to do it quietly, but I don't think I succeed because he pulls back just enough to look me in the eye.

"Try not to make too much noise," he murmurs. "You don't want to attract any attention, do you?"

At that moment something warm and supple snakes between my lower lips and I can't answer Kade, I can only groan helplessly as Lawson's tongue makes its way up me, from my pussy to my clit, where he laps at me in slow, perfect circles.

"*Oh*," I whisper as my whole body goes weak. I feel like a leaf falling from a tree, but Kade is there to catch me, supporting my body with his thick, muscled frame.

His hands are still down my shirt, my bra lifted over my breasts even though it's still secured around me as he pinches and rolls my nipples, softly then hard, then softly again. Lawson is licking me in long, slow, sensuous licks, like he wants to enjoy me slowly, taste everything that I've got to offer.

"He's busy right now, so it's up to me to tell you what we're going to do to you, peach," Kade murmurs into my ear, the sensation making me catch my breath, my nipples going even harder.

Lawson laps at my clit a little faster, one finger delving between my lips, teasing at the entrance to my pussy.

I whimper in pleasure.

"Right now he's going to lick you until your legs shake and I have to cover your mouth so you don't scream his name," he goes on. "We can't have you letting everyone know that you're with both your bosses in the conference room, can we?"

I mean to whisper *no, we can't*, but it just comes out as a quiet moan.

"Then it's my turn to taste your sweet honey, peach," he says. "I'm *dying* to feel you come with my tongue in your pussy."

Lawson's licking me faster and faster, his expert tongue driving me ruthlessly toward the edge as his finger pushes inside my virgin entrance, and I gasp.

In my ear, Kade chuckles.

"That's just the beginning, peach," he whispers. "The moment we get you back to our hotel room, we're going to take you properly. Don't worry, I promise it won't hurt. Just the opposite, in fact."

Now I've got one hand on Lawson's head, closed around his hair as he pushes my thighs apart, licking me furiously as he adds a second finger, crooking them both inside me and rubbing a pleasure spot inside my pussy that I didn't even know I had.

My back arches and I gasp loudly. *Too* loudly, because Kade pinches my nipples even harder but whispers in my ear again.

"Shh," he says, his voice low and teasing. "Peach, I haven't even told you how we're going to take turns fucking your tight little pussy and seeing who can make you come the hardest."

I bite my lip, groaning as Lawson's tongue doesn't stop. I'm right at the edge, ready to go over, both of my bosses playing my body expertly at once.

"You like the sound of that, don't you, peach?" he goes on as I writhe in his arms. "We're also going to share you, peach. Not tonight, but soon."

He kisses my neck, Lawson still lapping harder, faster, his fingers moving inside me.

"Share me?" I manage to squeak out, my voice barely a whisper.

He chuckles just as Lawson puts his lips around my clit and suddenly sucks. I nearly scream with pleasure, and in the nick of time, Kade puts one thick hand over my mouth, saving us.

"We're going to fuck you together," he whispers. "He's going to take your sweet little pussy and I'm going to fuck your tight little asshole."

I come.

61

I come so hard I bite Kade's finger as he presses his hand into my mouth to keep me from shouting and revealing what we're doing to everyone, because I feel like I've been hit by a rocket from outer space. Every muscle in my body tenses and jerks at once as I explode into a thousand little pieces, practically leaving my body behind.

Kade's whispering something else dirty in my ear but I can't even hear it. There are lights flashing in front of my eyes and I've got both hands knotted in Lawson's hair, pressing his face into me as hard as I possibly can.

The wave breaks over me again and again, far better and more intense than any solo orgasm I've ever had. My bosses just keep going, coaxing me on and up to newer heights until at last, I can't come any more.

I slacken my grip on Lawson's hair, slump in Kade's embrace. He finally takes his hand off my mouth though he's still supporting me from behind, taking me in his arms and kissing me on the temple, right by my ear.

"That was beautiful," he whispers. "The most beautiful thing I've ever seen."

Lawson pulls back, licking his fingers again as he removes them from me, dropping kisses on my inner thighs as he sits back, watching me.

"I've thought about that since the moment I saw you," he says, still licking his lips, his voice husky. "It was even better than I thought it'd be."

"You're not finished, are you, peach?" Kade asks me, as he slowly helps me sit up. "We're not finished yet. Don't you think it's unfair that he gets to taste you and I don't?"

Together, they pull me to standing, and Kade gets off the conference table behind me, giving me a long, lingering kiss before he does. Suddenly I'm sandwiched between them again, my leggings still around my ankles, as Kade's fingers explore me, sliding between my lips, just barely dipping inside as I moan into Lawson's mouth as he claims me.

Hands move over my body again, and I don't even know which man they belong to as they explore me with abandon, teasing my nipples, circling my clit as Kade pushes his fingers deeper yet.

Suddenly he pulls them out and I gasp in disappointment, only for him to move slowly, surely, to my puckered back hole.

My eyes go wide in surprise. I'm a virgin, and definitely *not* a technical virgin — the thought of someone touching *that* hole has barely ever occurred to me before, it's so filthy and forbidden.

But Kade groans into my ear, and I can feel his thick cock get even harder through his pants, and I feel my surprise waver, my eyes drifting shut.

It feels *good*, just to have his finger there, lightly circling it. It feels dirty and *wrong* — especially for my boss to be doing it, oh my *God* — but good anyway.

"Kade," I whisper as he keeps going, Lawson's lips now on my neck. "Oh, God, don't stop…"

But instead, both men suddenly stop moving. They go perfectly still in unison, and the only sound is suddenly my own breathing, ragged panting for breath.

"Was that—" Lawson says, his head snapping up before he can finish his sentence.

"It was," Kade finishes for him. "Better get dressed, peach."

I'm still dazed, my mind hazy from what just happened. But both men give me a quick kiss before Lawson pulls my leggings back up. I run one hand through my hair, still not sure what just happened — suddenly they're both professional as can be, picking up their briefcases and file folders, shoving my notepad into my hands — when the door opens.

Oh, *shit*. We're caught, we're definitely caught, totally busted because there's absolutely no way that anyone could open that door right now and not instantly know—

"Oh, sorry," says the woman who opened the door, a secretary of some kind with a generous figure and her blonde hair piled high in a bun. "I thought you'd left already."

I hold my breath, expecting her to do or say *something* that indicates she knows what just happened, but she doesn't.

"Just finishing up some unrelated business," Lawson says with a big, friendly smile, turning on the charm.

CHAPTER FOURTEEN

LAWSON

THE WOMAN WITH THE BUN PURSES HER LIPS, HER HAND STILL ON the doorknob of the heavy wooden door. I keep smiling, because even though the scent of sex is heavy in the air — and heavy on me as well, if she comes one step closer — I've never met a secretary I couldn't charm at least a little.

"We'll be out in just a moment," Kade says from somewhere behind me, his voice characteristically gruff and muted.

Jenna doesn't say anything. I don't dare look back at her right now, because I'm sure she looks like a deer caught in the headlights.

The secretary with the bun frowns.

"We do need this room within the next quarter hour," she says sternly, her accent brisk.

"Of course," I say. "Thank you *so* much for your patience."

She gives us all one good, long look, and it's the first time I get nervous. DiMaggio Holdings is a huge client, and if they were to find out what we were just doing in there they'd drop us in half a second, best lawyers in the business or not.

But instead she gives us a little shrug, turns, and lets the door shut behind her. Jenna lets out a huge sigh of relief, and when I turn, Kade's got an arm around her, a faint smile on his face even though Jenna looks like she's just escaped a bear attack.

"Rude of her to not say goodbye, don't you think?" I ask, trying to lighten the mood.

Jenna just swallows hard and tries to smile.

"That was really close," she says.

"I told you he could charm the spots off a leopard," Kade says.

He leans in to kiss her, briefly, and even though I'm right here, for half a moment my stomach swirls with jealousy.

I walk over, put my arm around her, and kiss her as well. Even now, *knowing* what could happen, my strongest urge is to yank down her leggings again and let her ride me in one of these leather executive chairs.

But I don't. For once, I behave myself.

"Come on," I say. "We've got that dinner in an hour and I think we all ought to shower, hm?"

Kade grins. Jenna looks down blushing, and as we leave the offices I'm fighting an erection at the thought of her, wet and slippery while we fuck.

BUT AT THE HOTEL, I keep behaving myself because I know how important this stupid dinner is, and I know what's going to happen *afterward*. So we all shower alone, and I put on the suit that the hotel's already pressed for me before heading downstairs to call a car.

Kade's already there — the man showers, shaves, and gets ready with military timing and precision, and I've never known him to be a minute late to anything, and while we're both standing in the lobby, trying to remember the names of the people we're about to see, the elevator doors open and Jenna walks out.

We both stop mid-sentence and stare. My mouth goes dry

and my cock springs to life as she walks toward us, hips swaying slightly in her heels.

"Let's cancel the dinner," Kade growls quietly so no one but me can hear. "Tell them we got the Black Death. They still got that here?"

I don't respond, just swallow hard. There's absolutely nothing that I want more than exactly that: forget dinner, and take Jenna right back upstairs.

It isn't as if she's wearing anything risqué or outwardly sexy: just a simple black dress that hugs her curves tastefully and ends just below her knee with heels, her long strawberry-blonde hair pinned up in a low bun. She's got bright red lipstick on her perfect, pillowy lips, and as she sees us staring, she blushes and worries her bottom lip between her teeth.

I growl softly, a sound no one but Kade can possibly hear, but I can't help it. When she does that, the only thing I can think about is those perfect, plush red lips wrapped around my cock as she looks up at me with her wide, innocent eyes, her mouth slowly engulfing my shaft as she moans slightly—

"We're all ready?" Jenna asks, her eyes flicking from me to Kade and back.

I blink, quickly coming back to reality and cursing myself for getting lost in fantasy like that.

Not now, Lawson, I remind myself. *Three hours.*

Be a lawyer for three damn hours and then she's yours.

"Of course," I say, still staring at her. Next to me, Kade is silent, but I know she can feel us undressing her with our eyes.

Even if I'd much, much rather be undressing her with my hands.

"Let's get this over with," Kade mutters, and turns for the lobby doors. Jenna quirks one eyebrow at me, not quite sure how to take this, so I smile gallantly at her and offer my arm.

"Forgive my friend, he's impatient," I joke.

"Oh?" she asks.

I glance around. It doesn't seem like anyone is watching us — and it's certainly not like any of our co-workers are here — so I bend down, put my lips to her ear for a moment.

"He'd much rather be having dessert first, peach," I murmur.

She glances up at me, her eyes round as another blush creeps onto her cheeks.

"You're dessert," I clarify in a whisper.

"I thought that might be the case," she says softly. "Let's get this dinner over with, then?"

I open the door for her and she steps through. Kade is there, phone out, standing on the curb as a limousine pulls up.

"That's us," he gruffs.

CHAPTER FIFTEEN

KADE

USUALLY, I LIKE THE FANCY DINNERS OUR CLIENTS INSIST ON. Hell, they're practically the only way I've been to the best restaurants in every city around the globe — if someone didn't force me to go, I'd probably spend all my time working, with the brief, occasional woman on the side.

And frankly, that's fine with me. I like working. I like my career, I like arguing in courtrooms, and I really like the power, prestige, and especially the money that comes with it.

Then I watched Jenna's perfect ass as she got into the limo, and absolutely none of that mattered.

I know I've got to go to this stupid dinner, because these men are paying us millions of dollars to make their claims in court, but it takes every ounce of self-control I have not to grab Jenna and drag her back to my hotel room, caveman-style.

Even though her outfit is perfectly businesslike and demure, somehow that only makes me want her more — knowing what my sweet peach is hiding beneath that facade.

Inside the limo, we share the back seat while Lawson sits opposite us. Jenna glances out the window, swallowing as she bites her lip.

Quickly, I check to make sure the partition's up, and I lean over to her ear as the limo pulls out of the hotel driveway.

"Make me a bet," I say, drawing my arm around her.

Jenna laughs quickly, glancing at Lawson and then me, a flush creeping down her neck. She tugs nervously at the hem of her dress, like she's trying to get it to cover her knees.

Lawson takes her hand, pushes it back up her thigh, and her laugh turns to a gasp of lust.

"What's the bet?" she whispers.

"The driver can't hear us, you know," Lawson says, voice friendly as ever, nodding at the partition. "Unless you get *really* loud."

He winks at her, and Jenna swallows, her fingers twisting in the hem of her dress.

"Why would I do that?" she teases.

"Take the bet and find out," I say, cock already straining against my pants. Holy *fuck* this dinner is going to be difficult.

Maybe if I just focus on how many chins our host has, or whether my filet mignon is properly medium-rare or not. Maybe *then* I can get this night over with and not make a complete ass of myself.

"You haven't told me what the bet is," she points out, tilting her head to one side.

"I bet I can make you come without taking your panties off," I tell her.

I slide my tongue along the outer shell of her ear, just for fun. Jenna gasps and I can feel the shudder that runs through her body.

"Come on, peach," I continue. "What were you expecting me to say? It sure as hell wasn't about intellectual property law."

She looks at me, eyes dark with lust. I have no idea how far away this fancy restaurant is, but I hope it's in fucking Scotland and we're driving all the way there tonight.

Jenna puts one hand on my knee, her fingers warm and light

through my pants. I thought I was hard already, but now my cock swells even more.

Jesus, this girl.

"And if you don't?" she murmurs.

"Then I have to make you come twice after dinner," I say.

Lawson's sitting on the bench seat opposite us, just watching, the outline of his cock obvious through his pants, his eyes glued to Jenna.

Good. Let him watch.

I put my hand under the hem of her skirt and slide it up her inner thigh, marveling at her soft skin under my fingers. Jenna's eyes go to half-mast and she exhales softly, looking up at me.

"You haven't taken the bet yet," I point out.

She clears her throat softly, obviously trying to focus.

"And if you win?" she asks softly.

"Then I get to make you come twice after dinner."

Lust hazes over her eyes, but she smiles a slight smile anyway.

"Sounds win-win," she says, her voice already breathy. "I accept."

"Good girl," I growl, and skim my fingers upward until I find the warm fabric of her panties, stroking my fingers along her.

She's already soaking wet, and as I faintly trace the outline of her lips through the thin cotton, Jenna moans quietly, dropping her head back against the seat of the limo and widening her knees just a bit.

Lawson's gaze is glued to the spot between her legs, even though he's sprawled casually along the seat opposite us.

"You're already wet as hell, peach," I murmur into her ear. "Is it true that all I've gotta do is talk a little dirty in your ear and you already can't help yourself."

"Maybe," she whispers.

I stroke her through her panties with my thumb, and she moans again, pushing her legs a little wider. I slide my fingers beneath the thin fabric without taking her panties off, and Jenna whimpers with desire.

"Does that mean I should keep talking dirty?" I ask. "I could tell you that nice girls don't get finger-fucked by one boss in the back of a car while the other boss watches. Or I could tell you that I fucking love how wet you are for us already, and that this dinner is going to be sheer total hell."

"I know," she moans.

I circle her clit with one finger for a moment, making her writhe on the back seat.

"Or I could tell you what we're going to do tonight," I say, rubbing her a little harder.

"What?" she gasps.

"First we're going to lick you until you come again," I say. "He's going to make you come with his tongue deep in your pussy while you put your pretty lips around my cock again, because I haven't been able to think about anything else since that plane ride."

Lawson stirs, swallowing hard, adjusting his pants as he does. He's half-smirking. I think he's enjoying the show, his eyes still glued to Jenna.

"And after we've satisfied you at least once, you're going to ride my cock with your pretty little pussy until you come again," I say, my lips brushing her ear as I speak.

Jenna just gasps, moaning, her head back against the seat behind her as I plunge two fingers into her tight entrance. I nearly moan myself at her wetness and tightness, moving my fingers in her channel until she moans again, the sound breathier than before.

"You're a dirty girl for a virgin, aren't you?" I whisper.

My only response is a gasp and a moan, her thighs parting even wider. Her skirt is hiked almost to her hips now, and Lawson's got a hungry look on his face as I bring Jenna even closer to the edge.

I hope we're stuck in traffic forever, and I hope we're not too close to the restaurant, because I'm loving torturing my sweet virgin girl like this, bringing her to the brink, Lawson watching, her totally under my power.

"Kade," she whisper-moans.

I push my fingers deeper, harder, my thumb circling her clit as I do. Jenna cries out, wordlessly, her whole body strung tight, ready to explode.

"Yes?" I tease.

"Kade," she whispers again. "Kade, make me—"

She cuts off, her eyes flashing open before sliding closed again.

"Make you what, peach?" I ask.

She doesn't respond, only pants for breath, biting her lip.

"You have to say it," I go on, working her faster, harder, feeling her body respond beneath my hand. "*Kade, make me come. Say it.*"

"Kade," she moans. "Make—"

The front door of the limo slams shut, and all three of us jump. I look out the tinted window, hand still deep in Jenna, and realize that we've come to a stop outside a building.

I also realize that there are footsteps outside. The driver coming to open the back door and let us out.

Jenna realizes it just as I do, and she *yelps*. I pull my hand out of her and she shoves her skirt back down, her face flushed, her knees slamming together as she gives me an embarrassed, panicked look.

I chuckle, and in the moment before the door opens, I lick her off my fingers. She's sweet and spicy and just fucking *perfect*.

"To be continued," I tell her, still licking. "I guess I lose, don't I?"

She opens her mouth to respond, but then the driver is there, the door open, holding out his hand for the lady. Lawson and I follow her out of the limousine and toward the lighted entrance of a *very* fancy restaurant.

Just before we go in, Lawson opens the restaurant door for her and uses the opportunity to whisper in her ear.

"Twice, peach," he says. "Just as soon as this is over."

God, I don't know if I can wait.

CHAPTER SIXTEEN

JENNA

THIS IS BY FAR THE FANCIEST RESTAURANT I'VE EVER BEEN IN. IT'S got some of the finest cuisine I've ever even been *near*, let alone eaten. We've got bottles of $200 wine out at the table, and it's flowing like water — even to me and the British assistant that the other team brought with them.

I should be having the time of my life right now, taking notes and savoring every moment to tell my similarly-poor friends back in New York.

But instead, I can't focus on *any* of that.

Because of Kade and Lawson. No matter how many delectable morsels I eat I can't get Kade's words out of my head.

You're going to ride my cock until you come.

God, every time I think that — about every thirty seconds — I get even wetter. I'm afraid to stand up from this chair, because I think I may have soaked right through my panties *and* my dress, but I can't stop thinking about it.

I can't stop thinking about the feeling of his fingers inside me. Just his *fingers* felt better than anything I could possibly imagine, taking me straight to heaven in the back of that limo.

I could have killed the driver when he opened that door,

because there's nothing that I wanted more than to stay exactly where I was.

But instead, now I'm *here*, in this very fancy restaurant, eating very fancy things, and wishing I was naked and sandwiched between both my bosses.

"More wine?" Niall, seated across from me, asks. There's already some wine in my glass, but I incline it toward him and accept another glug because my whole body is a vortex of nerves and desire.

"Thanks," I say nervously and take another sip, trying to act cool. Dinner's nearly over, and now we're just waiting on dessert — a chocolate souffle that one of the Brits at the table ordered in French. I didn't even know what he'd ordered until he told us all.

"Mind you don't drink too much," a smooth, velvety voice says in my ear, and I freeze instantly, my eyes going wide as I look around, praying that no one else is seeing Lawson talk to me this closely.

They're not.

"Why?" I whisper, still staring straight ahead into my wine glass.

Suddenly, his hand is on my knee, beneath the table, sparks shooting up my leg and straight to my pussy.

"We wouldn't want you to fall asleep too early," he goes on, his voice practically a purr. "We've got a much better dessert planned, peach."

Just at the sound of his voice, my pussy throbs. It's insane what's happened to me in the past few days — I went from a nice, normal assistant who thought her bosses were cute, to...

I blush, despite myself, remembering the scene on the airplane yesterday.

Or in the conference room today.

Or in the limo an hour ago.

Jesus.

Lawson's hand moves up my thigh even as his face turns away

from me, talking to the man on his other side. It's something business-related, but I'm not paying attention because of his fingers, steadily pushing their way between my clamped-shut thighs.

He's insistent. Determined, not about to take *no* for an answer.

Not that *no* is an answer I'm interested in giving, so I put my wine glass down, try to take a deep breath quietly, and open my knees under the table.

Instantly, his fingers are at my core, sliding against the soaked fabric of my thong. I bite my lips shut, forcing myself not to moan as he strokes me under the table, in the middle of the fanciest restaurant I've ever been in in my entire life.

Next to me, with his other hand, Lawson lifts his glass to his lips, saying something to the man on his other side while he pushes my panties aside underneath the table, his perfect, nimble fingers lightly dragging over my clit.

Inadvertently, I grab the stem of my wine glass, toes curling in my heels. He drags his fingers over my clit again and my lips part, a single, tiny exhalation coming out as I try to focus on the dessert fork that's still in front of me after the wait staff has cleared all the other dishes.

It's silver. Four tines.

Lawson dips one finger between my soaked lips then circles my clit with it, still pretending not to pay me any attention. I feel my face flush hard, and I keep on concentrating on the dessert fork.

It's... got a handle, I notice, as his fingers begin to move faster, harder.

I lock my feet around the rungs of my chair, trying to stay as still as I can. I can't *believe* I'm letting this happen, but I can't help myself. Not around these two men.

I can barely keep myself from writhing in this chair, grabbing the seat with my hands and leaning back, shouting and rolling my hips with pleasure. It's taking everything I've got not to moan Lawson's name right now, even if he's acting like nothing is going on, chatting business with the other men at the table.

His fingers keep moving, driving me to dizzying heights as my vision blurs with pleasure and I try to stay focused on the fork.

"Jenna."

It's... silver. On a tablecloth. It's fork-shaped.

"*Jenna.*"

My name rips me away, and for just a moment my lips part and a tiny, soft sound comes out, my hips just barely bucking of their own accord as Lawson's hand drives me higher and higher with pleasure.

Across the table, slightly catty-corner, is Kade, his eyes piercing through mine.

He knows, I realize.

Kade smiles, just barely. His gaze shifts until it's animal, almost feral, and even though he's at a fancy restaurant and wearing an incredibly expensive suit, I can tell he's having to control himself so he doesn't just tear it off.

"You all right, Jenna?" he murmurs.

I just nod, mutely. I'm close, *so* close, and my eyes and threatening to roll back in my head. On the table, my hands are shaking, so I hide them.

"You look..." Kade says, his voice dripping with suggestion, and he raises his eyebrows.

Lawson pinches my clit lightly between two fingers, and I gasp. I grab the stem of my wine glass again, bring my eyes to Kade's.

"I'm fine," I whisper, breath coming in quick, short, desperate pants.

"Maybe we should take you back to the hotel soon," he goes on, voice low and dark. "It's been a long day, I'm sure they won't mind."

I just nod. It's all I can do as Lawson's fingers work my clit even harder and faster. I bite my tongue between my teeth to keep myself from shouting, and I accidentally do it so hard that I taste blood.

Lawson's still pretending to ignore me, chatting with the person on his other side, but Kade is looking right at me, his intense eyes staring right into mine.

My lips part, just slightly. I grab my wine glass even harder, afraid I'm going to break the thin stem in my hand, but I need to grab onto *something* to anchor myself to reality right now.

I'm right on the brink, teetering on the edge. I can feel that my face is flushed bright red as I meet Kade's eyes, held under the spell of Lawson's perfect fingers, unable to do anything else.

He mouths something, across the table. My brain is blinking in and out with sheer pleasure, but then he mouths it again and suddenly I realize what he's saying.

Come for me.

I do. My whole body goes rigid and I close my eyes, grabbing my wine glass so hard that all my knuckles go white. It's a miracle it doesn't break in my hand as I come hard, wave after wave crashing against the shores of my body, Lawson's hand still moving and circling, coaxing every bit of pleasure from me that he can get.

When it's over I'm panting for breath, gasping. My whole body is trembling despite my best efforts, and as I open my eyes slowly, praying that the whole restaurant isn't staring at me, I feel a single trickle of perspiration slide down the back of my neck.

Subtly, Lawson's hand moves away as he finishes his conversation with the man on his other side. I can't stop watching as he glances down at it, in his lap, his eyes alight with a hunger I'm coming to understand all too well.

Quickly, so quickly I almost miss it, his tongue darts out over his lip, like he's tasting something delicious as he looks at me, a smirk on his face. Then he wipes his hand on his napkin, still below the table.

I come to my senses and close my legs so quickly that there's a sound as my thighs snap together in the middle, and I lift my wine glass to my lips and down the rest in a few gulps.

Across the table, Kade is still half-smiling, the wolfish look in his eyes still there as he takes a bite of his chocolate souffle.

I put my empty wine glass back down. I can't think about eating anything right now, my stomach in knots.

Not to mention the *other* parts of me. I'm well aware that this was only the prelude to tonight, and it's barely satiated my desire for what's coming. If that's what my two bosses can do to me at the table in a restaurant, I don't stand a chance later tonight.

Lawson leans in toward me, and the wine I just practically chugged sings through my veins.

"I'm afraid I'm feeling a bit jetlagged, to be honest," he says, partly to me and partly to the table as a whole. "I think the three of us might call it an early night."

The words send a bolt of heat straight down through my body, igniting me yet again. Kade glances at me, smiling.

"Yeah, I'm beat," he says.

I clear my throat, praying that I sound normal.

"I'm pretty tired as well," I say. "Flying in today and all. I think I've been awake for almost thirty-six hours!"

And I'm about to be awake for a couple more.

George and Niall both laugh and wave their hands.

"You mean you can't hold your liquor," George teases us, his British accent just a bit slurred. "Give you lot a few glasses of good wine and you're off for a nice nap. We'll be seeing you in the morning, have off!"

Kade and Lawson both stand, smiling, so I follow suit. I guess *have off* means 'feel free to leave,' because after shaking hands and bidding everyone farewell, that's exactly what we do.

CHAPTER SEVENTEEN

LAWSON

THE MOMENT WE'RE IN THE LIMO AGAIN, DOORS SHUT, I DRAG Jenna onto my lap. She yelps quietly, her body tense and rigid beneath my hands.

"You can't tell me you're surprised," I murmur into her ear. "Not after you just came in front of everyone in Le Chevalier."

Her breath quickens. On the other seat, across from us, Kade leans forward, smiling.

"You know you don't get her twice in a row, don't you?" he says, his voice a deep growl.

I grab Jenna's hips in my hands and pull her down, harder. Her dress is already hiked over her panties, so all that separates my throbbing cock from her sweet, wet pussy is a few layers of cloth.

"I didn't see you make her come back there," I tease him, pulling her against my thick cock again.

Jenna moans softly, her body a little unsteady in my hands. One more time her hips writhe against me, her perfect ass moving in a slow grind as she leans forward, putting her palms on my knees.

I slide my fingers under the back of her thong against the bare skin of her hips as Kade leans forward.

"Peach," he says, his face an inch from hers. "Which of us do you want to fuck first?"

My cock twitches hard at the phrase, at the thought of being buried in her tight little pussy.

"Do I have to choose?" she murmurs, flexing her hips again. I squeeze the globes of her ass in my hands, my fingers digging into her perfect, firm flesh even as the hunger inside me reaches epic proportions.

"I know you want us both, you sweet filthy thing," I say. "But I'm afraid we can't *both* fuck you at the same time."

I dig my fingers in harder, sliding the pad of one thumb between her cheeks until it just barely brushes over the delicate nub there.

She gasps.

"Not yet, at least," I go on. "You're still a virgin, peach, we're going to start you out slow."

"Slow and hard," Kade promises, leaning in more.

He slides one hand around her face, cupping the back of her head in his palm, his fingers laced through her hair, undoing the low bun it was twisted into.

"You can have us both later," I promise her, grinding her hips against my swollen cock one more time, barely biting back a moan myself. "Though if you keep asking us like that, I'm not sure how long we can hold out."

"You'll have us both soon enough, peach," Kade says, and then his mouth is on hers in a rough, claiming kiss.

I should hate watching this. I should, but I don't, because of the way her body moves when he kisses her, hips rolling against me in a show of pure desire. I don't mind sharing Jenna with Kade — *only* with Kade — because of the way she's already overwhelmed with desire and pleasure.

That alone makes this worth it.

I move my hands down, dip one finger into her pussy. She's soaking wet, so wet that the crotch of my suit is going to be wet with her juices when she stands up, but I don't mind.

Hell, I might never wash it again.

Jenna moans again, the sound breathy and ethereal in the tight space of the car.

"Kade," she murmurs, then swallows. "Lawson, we shouldn't—"

I just laugh as suddenly, the limo pulls to a stop and I take my hands off her, pull her dress down.

"Don't start that nonsense now," I tell her. "Don't you think it's a little bit late for that?"

When the door opens, she's sitting on the seat again, demure as ever, even though I was right and there's a wet spot where she was sitting on my suit.

"You know I'm right," she says quietly, her eyes sparking. "We shouldn't, but we're going to anyway."

With that, Jenna gets out of the limousine, the driver offering her one hand. Kade and I follow, and I don't even bother to try hiding the spot where she sat on me or the obvious, massive, *aching* erection I've got going on right below it.

We cross the lobby, one on either side of her, without speaking. To be honest I can't think of anything to say that isn't *completely* fucking filthy. I want to say *I'm going to fuck your brains out, peach*, and I want to say *you're going to take my cock as deep as you can until you come all over it*, and I want to say *I can't wait to watch you suck Kade's cock again.*

None of that is much good for polite society.

The elevator is crowded. An older lady wearing a neck full of pearls glances at my cock, then frowns at me. I grin at her, because I can't help it, thinking *that's right, lady. I'm gonna go upstairs and fuck this sweet young thing.*

When we get to his room, Kade's got it open in half a second. The room's got a massive king bed, a couple of sumptuous, overstuffed chairs, and a breathtaking view of London below, but none of us are paying attention to any of that.

Inside, the door slams shut. There's a single lamp on somewhere, and I whirl Jenna around, take her chin in one hand and tilt her up to face me.

"Say it again," I growl.

She blinks, then half-smiles, like she's teasing me.

"Say what?"

"That you want to fuck us both."

"I never actually said that, you know," she teases.

I run the pad of one thumb over her hips as Kade steps up behind her, already lifting the hem of her dress up over her thighs, exposing her to both of us.

"Don't play coy, peach," he growls, hooking his thumbs under her thong.

"Then say it for the first time," I tell her.

Jenna looks at me, pure fire in her eyes, then sucks my thumb into her mouth and runs her tongue along the pad, moaning softly as she does.

I growl, the sound rising involuntarily from the pit of my chest. There's the sound of a zipper going down as Kade undoes her dress from the back, and she pulls my thumb from her mouth as his hands move inside her dress, eyelids fluttering.

I pull at her dress, and now she's nearly naked as it falls off, in just her bra and thong. We make short of work of the bra, and I take her full, perky breasts in my hands and run my open palms over her nipples before taking them between my fingers and pinching them until she gasps.

"Say it," I command.

Her eyes are shut, and her hands drift over my shoulders, her back arched with pleasure and anticipation.

"I want to fuck you both," she breathes.

CHAPTER EIGHTEEN

KADE

I CAN'T WAIT ANY LONGER FOR HER. I KNOW IT'S A BIT RUDE TO skip foreplay, but for fuck's sake, the past day has been nothing but foreplay. Every time she looks at us, every time she moves, every time she opens her mouth I just want her more and more.

"Good thing, peach," I growl in her ear. "Your dirty fantasies are just about to come true."

My fingers dig into her hips as I nip at her neck, biting her delicate skin just a little bit too hard, because I can't help myself around her. On her other side, Lawson is still rolling her nipples between his fingers, and Jenna's moaning quietly.

I push her dress down off her hips, and pull at one side of her thong until it snaps in my hand, then toss it on the floor. Jenna gasps and looks over her shoulder at me, her eyes blazing with lust and just a little uncertainty, so I slide one hand into her wetness and instantly, her body yields to me.

"Don't worry, peach," I murmur. "I can be gentle, too."

Then we're on the bed, Jenna on her back, and now I'm standing between her legs, leaning over her perfect, naked body and claiming her mouth. I plunder her, letting my hands roam everywhere while she tugs at my shirt, my belt.

I get them off instantly, watching the rise and fall of her chest as I do, her big eyes pleading with me for more. She's borderline desperate for this, my sweet, beautiful virgin.

Our virgin.

The moment I'm stripped naked, Jenna reaches down and grabs my cock in one hand, stroking it from root to tip. I brace myself on my forearms over her, a deep rumble escaping my chest as she bites her lip, eyes searching mine.

"You like it, don't you?" I say, barely aware of Lawson, also on the bed, clothes shed. "You like the thought of having your cherry popped by your boss's thick cock."

She blushes. She's naked on a bed with two men, my cock in her hand, and Jenna *blushes*.

It's hot as fuck. Lawson chuckles, and as he does, Jenna reaches her other hand up and grabs his cock as well, changing his laughter to a moan in an instant.

That's it. I can't take this anymore, this teasing, flirting, coy virgin. I need her, *right* now, or I might lose my mind.

I grab my cock, moving her hand, and slide it down her seam and to her slick entrance, making her moan again as I pass her clit. Jenna closes her eyes, panting for breath, Lawson's cock still in her other hand as she grabs my hips like she's trying to draw me inside her, but instead, I pause a moment.

I want to savor this, the last time I'll ever fuck a virgin. Because I can't imagine having other women after Jenna — even now, somehow, I know she's my last.

"Kade," she whisper-moans, her hips rolling, her fingers digging into the flesh on my side. "Please."

That's all I need, and I push the tip of my cock inside her, stretching the entrance of her virgin pussy around me.

Instantly, Jenna gasps, her whole body tensing even though I'm barely inside her. She's tight as hell, the sensation so intense that for a moment I'm nearly overwhelmed.

Lawson leans down and kisses her deeply, his fingers pinching one nipple.

"It'll only hurt for a moment, peach," he murmurs into her mouth. "Promise."

She kisses him back, and slowly, her body relaxes. Her hips move again, her legs wrapped loosely around my waist, and I lean forward, sliding more of my thick length inside her.

I feel something give. Jenna gasps again, her hands clenching the sheets, as Lawson kisses her again, deeply, one of his hands moving down her body until his fingers are circling her clit.

"Fuck, peach," I murmur, forcing myself still until she relaxes again. "You feel fucking perfect."

Gradually, her breathing eases. She relaxes, her hands unclenching. Her hips move again, inviting me deeper, as Lawson massages her clit in slow, steady circles. I've got both hands on her thighs, holding them around me, and I'm practically trembling with the force of resistance.

I want *desperately* to fuck her hard and fast and deep right now, right here, Jenna's readiness be damned. I *need* to feel every inch of her, *need* to be deep inside her until she comes screaming our names.

And I will. Dear God, I will, but right now she needs me to be patient. Gentle.

"More," Jenna whispers.

I give her more, slowly, millimeter by incredible millimeter until I'm sunk deep inside her, my grip tight on her knees while she gasps and moans.

"More," she gasps again, her hands scrabbling at my hips. "God, please, Kade, *more*."

I grab her hips hard and tug her down, hilting myself and leaning in, over her body.

"Don't stop," Jenna moans. "Please don't stop, *please*."

"You want more?" I ask, my voice rough with forced self-control. "*This* isn't enough, peach?"

She writhes, moving my cock inside her, and her back arches as my hard length hits every pleasure center. Already I can feel her muscles starting to spasm and tighten around me, her breath coming in short ragged gasps.

And she wants *more*. I can give her more.

I pull out, slowly, fuck my sweet peach again, a little faster and harder than the first time. Lawson's still got his fingers on her clit and she's got one hand on his shoulder now, her nails digging into his muscles while she moans.

I fuck her again. Harder, faster, and even though I was determined that her first time would be easy, gentle, *soft*, this is quickly becoming anything but. With every stroke I'm driving as deep as I can, giving her the *more* that she wants, and Jenna's reacting like a woman who's caught fire.

I grit my teeth together, fingers digging into her legs. I'm determined not to come yet, not until she does, no matter how sweet and tight her pussy is.

No matter how fucking beautiful she is like this, spread in front of us, gasping with the pleasure we're giving her.

Jenna's hand finds Lawson's cock, and blindly, she starts stroking it with the same cadence I'm fucking her with. He growls, the noise coming from deep in his chest, his fingers on her clit moving faster and harder.

"Don't come yet," he tells her. "Don't you *dare* come yet, you filthy girl, I want to watch you like this—"

"Lawson," she moans, her eyelids fluttering.

I fuck her again, hard, and I make sure to hit the spot I *know* is driving her insane. Her pussy grips me like a fist, and I nearly come right then, despite myself.

"Don't come," he says again, his voice low and playful and teasing.

"I'm trying," she whimpers, his cock still in her fist. "I'm trying, but I can't— Lawson, it feels so *good*, I can't help it..."

I fuck her one more time and Jenna just *explodes*. She clamps down around me so hard I nearly come, white filtering in from the edge of my vision. I lean over the bed, gasping, but I don't stop. I just keep fucking her hard and deep while she comes and comes, shouting and moaning, begging us not to stop over and over again.

So we don't stop.

"Kade," Jenna gasps, her body still shuddering. "Oh my God, Kade, that was..."

She stops, looks up at Lawson. She bites her lip, and I fuck her again, slowly. She moans, her eyes sliding shut for a moment.

"That felt so good," she whispers.

Lawson kisses her, fingers still lazily circling her clit, her muscles still jolting every few second.

"That was round one," he murmurs.

CHAPTER NINETEEN

JENNA

Round one?

I look up at Lawson, his blue eyes boring into mine. I came so hard I can barely think, and I don't know what he means by *round one*.

I can only pant for breath, lying on my back, Kade still rock-hard inside me, his thick cock practically thrumming with heat, desire and lust and want still yawning inside me, like a bottom-less pit.

Lawson growls, his hand moving off of my clit, tracing a trail of my own wetness up my body until he's pinching a nipple, my scent wafting up to my nose.

"You're so fucking beautiful when you come," he says, his lips hovering over mine. "I hope you're ready to do it again, peach, because we're just getting started."

Oh. That's what they mean by *round one*. Of course.

I bite my lip, still looking up at him. I don't know how to answer that, because I can't even find words for the dirty things I want my bosses to do to me, and despite everything I don't think I'm brave enough to say them out loud.

"Yes," is all I manage to say, my voice coming out breathy, almost seductive.

The moment I say it Lawson captures my mouth with his, just as Kade suddenly pulls out. I protest into Lawson's mouth, suddenly empty and bereft, and he pulls back, chuckling.

"Are you *that* eager for more cock, peach?" he asks, grinning. "You're an insatiable little minx, aren't you?"

With that he moves down my body, planting kisses between my breasts, on my belly, and I hold my breath as he works his way down my abdomen, pausing above my mound.

My toes curl with anticipation, and I look up, at the edge of the bed, into Kade's burning eyes and nearly gasp.

Somehow, I haven't actually seen him naked before, not in all his glory like this, and he's *breathtaking*. The man looks good in a suit, sure, but he looks so good *out* of a suit that heat twists inside me yet again and my toes curl at the sight of his big, thickly muscled body, the way he's standing there as casual as can be.

I don't have as good of a view of Lawson but I can see the dim light playing on his muscles too, long and lean and rippling darkly as he bends over me, teasing me. *Torturing* me.

My gaze falls further and lands on Kade's cock. Jesus, I still can't believe that thing was *inside* me.

I can't believe that thing *took my virginity*.

I can't believe how hard it made me come, and I can't believe how ready I am to do it again. With another man — my other boss — who's standing right here, who watched everything.

"Please," I whisper again, heat and desire twisting and unfurling inside me, sending tendrils through my core and limbs until I almost can't stand it.

"*Please*," I start begging. "Please, Lawson, I need you."

Laughing, he lowers his head between my legs. I twist my fingers through his hair as he hoists my thighs onto my shoulders, his thick, sensuous lips brushing softly against my clit.

My whole body jolts and I gasp with the light pressure, hands knotting in his hair.

Then I feel his tongue, teasing me even more, softly running between my lips, just *barely* licking my entrance between them.

I whimper. My eyes are closed and my head is back, and I don't even see Kade as he walks around the side of the bed, cock still dripping with my juices. I only feel his weight when he's suddenly right next to me, on his knees, looking down.

Just as I open my eyes again to see Kade's proud, thick cock standing at attention, Lawson suddenly backs up a few inches, his hands curled around my hips.

"Tell me something, peach," he says, his voice slow and lazy, laconic but still sexy as hell. "Don't you find missionary a little bit boring?"

I swallow, looking up into Kade's eyes. I've only done missionary exactly once and *boring* was the last thing I thought it was, but the words won't enter my mouth.

"I've got no comparison," I manage to finally breathe out, just as his tongue lavishes its attentions once more on my clit, sliding slowly downward, between my lips, over my tight opening.

And then even *further* downward, to my puckered back hole, and suddenly I'm gasping and squirming as he circles it once, twice, white-hot rockets of forbidden pleasure shooting through my body.

Then he stops. Looks up at me and grins.

"Guess we'll have to give you a basis for comparison, then," he says.

Before I know what's happening Lawson's grabbed both my thighs and used them to flip me around so I'm on my stomach, arms folded under me.

"Oh!" I yelp, but already he's pushing me further onto the bed and I bring my knees and hands underneath me, pushing myself up.

Kade is there, and he puts one hand under my chin, lifting it. I swallow hard, Lawson's weight now on the bed behind me, his thick, rough hands palming my ass, grabbing me in the crease between my thighs and hips.

Kade kisses me, hard and slow, his tongue invading my mouth as Lawson's fingers find my clit. He strokes me once and I moan into Kade's mouth before he slides them back, over my swollen, wanting pussy, and to a quick, small circle of my tight back hole before he stops.

Then it's his cock. I'm still kissing Kade ferociously, *desperately* as Lawson's cock finds my entrance and he hilts himself in one single deep, hard stroke, instantly igniting all my pleasure centers and making me shout into Kade's mouth, the kiss suddenly over.

Lawson groans, his hips rocking against my ass as he pushes against me, like he's trying to get even deeper. There are stars on the edges of my vision now, and I realize that Kade's hand is in my hair, gently holding my head back as I look up at him.

"You're so fucking tight, peach," Lawson growls. "Your sweet little pussy fits me like a glove."

"Fuck me," I gasp out, the only words that I can think of right now, the deep, insatiable *need* for him overcoming all my mental faculties.

Then Kade's cock is there, in front of my face, and without thinking twice I open my mouth, already hungry for him as his hand guides my head back, hair still fisted in his hand.

There's no foreplay, I just suck him into my mouth as deeply as I can, the tip of his thick cock hitting the back of my mouth almost instantly, his taste musky and salty on my tongue.

Above me, Kade groans, his hand going even tighter in my hair, a few tears forming in my eyes as I slurp him out, swirling my tongue around his shaft as I do.

"You're so fucking sexy, peach," Kade sighs as I rock backward into Lawson, his cock still buried deep in my pussy. I feel like there's an electrical charge passing between the two of them, straight through my body. Like I'm some sort of erotic conduit.

Behind me, Lawson just groans, his hands palming my ass as he does, the sound full of pure lust and barely-held restraint.

"I can't last long like this, peach," he growls behind me.

Slowly, he pulls his cock out and I shudder with every millimeter. It's perfect, exquisite torture, and his hands are there, holding me steady. Forcing me to stay still, not rock back and take him again like I desperately want to.

Instead I push my head down on Kade's cock again, wanting, *needing* to have at least one of them inside me. I take him as far as I can, the head of his cock against the back of my mouth even though my lips are only halfway down his shaft.

Lawson pulls out, the head of his cock waiting at my entrance. My whole body quivers with desire, with *want*.

"Relax your throat," Kade whispers above me. "Swallow my cock like a good girl."

I take a deep breath through my nose, steeling myself. I've never done anything like this before — I've only put my mouth on a dick one other time, and that pales in comparison — so I'm nervous, but I obey.

I relax my hands, open my mouth, try to relax my throat. My eyes tear up a little as I lean forward, trying to take Kade's massive width even deeper, trying to swallow him like I so desperately want to, hear the way he'll groan with pleasure when I do—

Just then Lawson fucks me again, and this time isn't gentle or slow, it's *hard* and deep and I groan loudly onto Kade's cock.

Then suddenly I'm swallowing him, the thick head slipping effortlessly into my throat and Kade moans explosively.

"Jesus, peach," he says, panting for breath. "That feels *incredible.*"

"Do you know how fucking sexy you look?" Lawson pants behind me. "With me fucking you while you suck his cock?"

He fucks me again, and every pleasure center in my whole body lights up at once, like fireworks. Kade pulls out and I suck him desperately as he does, slurping his cock from my mouth, tongue lavishing over the end for a heartbeat before I gasp and plunge my lips back down.

I want them both inside me. I *need* them both, even though this breaks every rule I have. I want to show them — my *bosses* — as much pleasure as they've shown me.

I want to be their secret, dirty girl. I want to let them take total control over me, over my body, use me for their pleasure however they want.

But I can't deny that it feels good, absolutely *incredible.* Lawson fucks me deeper, harder, faster, and I moan into Kade's cock, slurping and swallowing, pushing him as deep as I possibly can while his hand is tight in my hair, guiding me up and down.

Lawson's got both hands on my hips, slamming me back into him as he fucks me hard, my knees wide on the comforter. I'm panting for breath in time with Kade's cock, completely out of my senses with pure pleasure.

"You're gonna make me come, peach," Kade growls. He's got his head thrown back, his hips thrusting shallowly toward me, my nose buried in the short hair at the base of his cock.

He pulses in my throat and I push him in further, my hands making fists in the comforter of the hotel bed.

Lawson keeps fucking me, hitting my pleasure spots over and over again, his cock perfect with every single thrust. I can feel my climax building, threatening to break free at any second.

"Come for us, dirty girl," Lawson growls, his voice deeper and rougher than ever. "Show us how much you like taking two cocks at once, peach."

I moan but the sound is cut short because I swallow Kade again, hard and deep, pressing my nose to his skin and feeling the shudder of pleasure that runs through his body.

It runs through mine, too, and then there's a slow chain reaction that goes off inside me as Lawson fucks me hard one more time.

He sets me alight, like the fuse on dynamite, the spark deep in my pussy that travels through my body in waves of pleasure until they all hit me at once. I cry out, the sound humming through Kade's cock still in my mouth, my whole body shaking as I come even harder than before.

My vision goes white, and suddenly there's nothing in this world except the three of us, fucking on this bed, as pleasure wracks my body from end to end, lighting every nerve on fire as I come.

Behind me Lawson groans, holding me tight against him as suddenly his body jerks and his cock pulses. I can feel him come inside me, still buried deep, and I push myself backward. I want as much of him as I can take, every drop he has to give me, and I suck Kade greedily at the same time.

Moments later, he explodes too, and I swallow him again and again as he does. I'm completely and utterly in the moment, nothing but pure physical desire, acting out of sheer lustful instinct.

After a moment, Kade pulls back, his cock starting to soften. I gasp for air, his hand relaxing in my hair, and look up at him.

He slides one thumb across my cheekbone, the gesture gentle, almost...

...it's almost loving. The last thing I expected after what just happened, while I'm still on my hands and knees, but then Lawson pulls out as well. I can feel him seep out and down the inside of my thigh, and before I know it he's bending over me, planting a quick, tender kiss between my shoulder blades.

"You're so fucking beautiful right now," Kade murmurs, and I blink up at him.

It's not what I was expecting. I thought he'd say something dirty right now, and I'd gasp and blush and probably get turned on all over again, but his voice is perfectly sincere.

Gentle, even.

"You're ours, aren't you, peach?" Lawson murmurs from behind me.

Slowly, he pulls me back, until I'm sitting, and wraps his arms around me from behind. We're both sweaty, but neither of us cares. I lean my head back against his thick, muscled frame, and Kade moves over until he's on my other side.

Kade kisses me on the temple, his hand on my leg. Everything feels warm and fuzzy, and I'm suddenly so tired and out of it that I can barely keep my eyes open so I relax into their arms.

"Of course I'm yours," I murmur, my voice suddenly soft in the huge hotel room overlooking the London skyline. "Of course."

Now it's Lawson's turn to kiss my forehead, the gesture loving and protective and sexy all at once. If I weren't so dazed by what just happened, I think I'd be stunned and probably worried.

Because I shouldn't be here. I shouldn't have just slept with my bosses.

At the same time.

On a business trip.

Everything about this spells trouble, clear as day, but despite that I know one thing.

I'm absolutely going to do it again.

CHAPTER TWENTY

LAWSON

The next morning, I wake up impossibly early. The hotel room has blackout curtains, like all hotel rooms, but even around the edges I can just barely see the first light of dawn creeping through in tones of hushed violet.

I have no idea what time it is, but the instant I wake up, my mind starts whirring. I'm in London. I've got work to do, deadlines to meet, I've got to make sure that every I is dotted and every t is crossed because DiMaggio Holdings is a stickler for details, and with the amount of money they're paying the firm?

I need to be too.

I lean myself up on one elbow, just to look at the clock, but when I do something moves in the bed next to me and I freeze.

I blink in the dark.

Then Jenna rolls over, onto her back, her strawberry-blonde hair fanning around her head, and the memory cuts through the fog of my morning brain and I remember *instantly*.

Last night. Her with the two of us, taking us both at once. How fucking sexy she looked on her back, tits bouncing as she gasped with pleasure, coming while Kade fucked her hard and deep. How beautiful she was when she came that way, how I loved getting to watch her.

How incredible it was to finally be inside her, feeling her tight pussy clench and grasp at me, driving her closer and closer to climax until finally I couldn't hold on any longer and spilled myself inside her while Kade did the same thing, feeling the delicious shudder of her body below mine.

And then, the three of us falling asleep together, Jenna in the middle, sandwiched between us.

We shouldn't have stayed here, like this. They should have left, because what if someone calls their rooms and they're not there?

God forbid, what if someone stops by looking for one of them?

We'd be fucked, and not the good kind either.

But then Jenna's eyes flutter open and she stretches, her perfect curves rubbing against me in the massive bed the three of us are sharing, and instantly I forget all about how this could cost me everything.

Because all I can think about is *her*, blinking up at me for a long moment, like she's trying to remember what I'm doing in her bed.

Then her eyes flick down, like she's embarrassed. Clearly, she's remembered.

"Jetlag?" she asks softly. "What time is it?"

I steady one hand on her hip and raise my head, checking the clock behind Kade's slumbering form, on the other side of Jenna.

"It's not even six yet," I say, stroking her naked hip below the covers. "Early, even for me."

"You travel a lot," she says, still keeping her voice quiet. "You must know some good tricks to get rid of jet lag, right?"

She smiles at me, rolls onto her side. Now her skin is warm against mine, shooting spikes of desire straight through my body.

I'm already stiff as a plank, the swollen tip of my cock rubbing against the front of her thighs.

I didn't mean for this to happen. I meant to get out of bed early, grab some coffee, and go over briefs until it was time to head to the office.

But now that it's started, there's a zero percent chance I'm going to stop.

"I know one good trick," I say, my hand finding the small of her back. I pull her closer, her soft skin warm under the blankets, and I press her against me, cock at full attention as her eyes briefly go wide.

"What's that?" Jenna whispers, one hand against my chest.

She nuzzles my calf with one foot, resting against the outside of my ankle, her knee just barely grazing my thigh.

"A quick morning fuck," I tell her, grinning wolfishly.

She laughs too, her voice soft in the dim light, and she looks down again, her hand still on my chest. Behind her, Kade stirs, turns onto his side, and then stops moving. The man has always been able to sleep like a log, and moreover, I don't think jetlag affects him.

It's unfair as all hell. Or at least it *was*, until right now, when I nestle one fingertip in the hollow of Jenna's throat and draw it slowly downward, between her breasts, and over her bellybutton. I slide it between her legs, nestle it against her clit, just *barely* moving it.

Her eyes close and she moans, ever so softly.

"I can't verify this," I say, wiggling my fingertip and eliciting a shudder of pleasure from her, "But I have it on excellent authority that taking a hard ride on a big cock will cure you of jetlag, *instantly*."

Her eyes dim as I move my finger against her clit again, her breathing going shallow, the haze of lust settling over her. It's all I can do not to lick my lips, just watching her like this.

Hands down, it's the world's best way to wake up.

She moans softly, eyes half-closed, lips parted. On the other side of her Kade stirs again, slightly, then settles back down as Jenna's hand slides over my rock-hard chest, her fingers feeling through the bulges and dimples of muscle.

I slide another finger between her legs so her clit is not between them, and I close my fingers ever so softly, still rubbing. Even though I'm not touching her pussy I can feel her wetness already, and I can feel the way she wants *more*, bucking her hips gently against me while I rub her.

It might be unfair to Kade, but the man could sleep through a hurricane. It's not my fault if he stays asleep through this whole thing.

Jenna's sliding her knee up my thigh, her hand now on my bicep, opening herself more and more to me with every passing second. I'm hard as a steel rod, my cock brushing against her inner thigh, and every time it does she rolls her hips just a little, her whole body moving in a perfect, slow rhythm.

"Well, peach," I say, still rubbing her clit between my fingers, watching her glorious body move with my ministrations. "What's it going to be?"

She swallows, her eyes barely open as she looks up at me, eyelashes aflutter.

"What?" she breathes, as if it's hard for her to concentrate.

"Are you gonna tease me all morning, or are you gonna ride my cock?" I ask with a grin.

Jenna opens her mouth to answer but I don't let her. I already know the answer, I just want to capture her mouth with mine, feel her melt into me, a puddle of desire. I bite her bottom lip between my teeth just hard enough for her to make a noise before I pull back.

With one quick motion I roll onto my back, pulling Jenna on top of me.

"Oh!" she exclaims, briefly off-balance, using her hand on her chest to steady herself.

"Trick question," I say, her hips already in my hands. "We both know what the answer is, peach."

There's a moment of uncertainty in her eyes, but then my girl arches forward, one hand already wrapped around my cock, her other hand on my chest. She's still a little unstable, but I've got her tight as she rises up onto her knees, brushing my cock against her entrance.

I growl at her, fingers digging into her hips, and she smiles slightly. Like she's teasing me, her tight wetness against my tip utterly *tantalizing*.

"Come on, peach," I say, my voice coming out low and lust-rough. "Why don't you—"

She cuts me off by sliding down my cock all at once, hilting me deep on the first stroke, and my words turn into a loud groan. Jenna gasps, her hand on my chest balling into a fist, her lips parting and her eyes closing.

Fuck, she feels good. She feels *amazing*, like she's custom-made to fit my cock, tight and wet, pulsing with desire.

"You dreamed about this, didn't you?" I ask, keeping my voice low and my hands on her hips, moving her back and forth slightly. "That's why you woke up so hot and bothered and ready to go, because we were fucking in your dreams."

Even though she doesn't respond right away, the look in her eyes tells me I'm right. That look, along with the way she grinds down onto me, her clit against my skin as my cock moves inside her, the sweet ache of pleasure building inside me.

"Maybe," she finally breathes, letting her fingers unfurl on my chest.

"Did it feel this good in your dream?" I ask, moving her hips again.

She responds by moaning quietly, a breathy little sound, and she starts to ride me. Jenna's uncertain at first, a little off-balance, but slowly, she moves faster, harder. She takes me all the way deep with every stroke, and before long I'm clenching her thighs in my hands, forcing myself not to come before she does.

I may be dirty as hell, but I'm a fucking gentleman, so I grind my teeth together and watch the way her perfect tits bounce up and down, the pattern mesmerizing.

"You like being stuffed full of cock first thing in the morning?" I ask her, even though I already know the answer.

From the way her eyes are unfocused, from the way she's biting her lip and turning a beautiful shade of orgasmic pink, from the way she's grinding her clit against my hips with every stroke, I can tell she *loves* this. But I want to hear her say it.

But Jenna just moans, both her hands on my stomach, like she's trying to keep her balance, so I pull her down harder, push her clit against me with my cock deep inside her. I have to force myself not to come, but I don't.

"Say it," I growl. "Tell me, peach."

Something like laughter flickers through her eyes, but only for a moment as I shift her hips with my hands and she moans again, helplessly.

"I like it," she breathes, her voice hitching with desire. "I like being— being stuffed full of cock."

"Good," Kade's voice says suddenly, off to my left.

Jenna and I both turn our heads instantly, looking over at my best friend and business partner, still in the bed with us. Even though he just woke up, he's grinning, his hands behind his head, clearly enjoying the show.

"Good lord, don't stop on my account," he says. "My own fault for sleeping in."

CHAPTER TWENTY-ONE

KADE

THIS?

This is the third-best way a man could possibly wake up, in my estimation.

The first, obviously, would be to wake up already buried in Jenna's tight little pussy, eyes coming open to see my gloriously sexy assistant riding me like she's riding Lawson right now.

Second best would be waking up with my cock down her throat, her innocent-but-hungry eyes looking up at me as she sucked me off as a good morning.

But this is third. Watching our sweet angel coming apart, getting properly fucked by the only other man I trust to do a good job of it, is pretty good.

They start again, Jenna slowly bucking her hips back and forth, finding the rhythm that they'd lost a moment ago. She's still slow, tentative, far from an expert, but I know all that will change in the next few weeks.

Her gaze keeps flicking from Lawson to me, back and forth, like she's not quite sure what to do now that she has an audience, even though she's still riding his cock like she can't help herself.

I grin again, put my hand on her thigh, slowly move it upward to where my best friend is fucking her.

"Come on, peach," I say. "Aren't you going to let us watch you come?"

I find her clit with my fingers, circle them around her small, swollen nub as she moans with pleasure. Lawson tugs on her hips again, arching himself off the bed as he fucks her slow and hard, a groan escaping Jenna's lips as he hilts himself. I've got the perfect view of their union, and I'm hard as a fucking rock watching his thick shaft pulse into her pretty pink pussy.

"Kade," she whispers, her eyes at half-mast. "I didn't know you were…"

I sit up onto my knees beside her, still rubbing her clit, and lean into her ear.

"You didn't know I was right next to you?" I tease, sliding my other hand down her arm, taking her hand. "You didn't think I'd wake up when you started riding Lawson's cock and moaning loud enough to wake the Queen?"

I don't wait for her to answer, but I take her hand and wrap it around my own thick shaft, groaning involuntarily as she pumps me once, still riding Lawson.

I get behind her, straddling Lawson's legs as well, her hand still around my cock as I massage her clit even harder. Now she's between us, facing him, but the three of us are moving together like we're all fucking.

Soon.

I bite my lip as she pumps me again, taking Lawson's big cock with a near-orgasmic shudder. It's all I can do to stop myself from leaning her forward, pushing my fingers knuckle-deep into her tender back hole, making her gasp and groan with new pleasures.

I squeeze my hand into a fist on her hip as she takes him again, her fingers sliding down my cock and her body starts quivering, a shallow gasp coming from her mouth. I know she's close, right on the brink, so I lower my lips to her neck and suck at the soft skin there, even as I try not to think about what I really *want* to do.

What I *really* want is to bend her slightly forward, take her hair in one hand, and slide my cock into her puckered back hole. I'd go slow — the first time at least — but being inside her, together with Lawson?

Both of us fucking her senseless, making Jenna come until she can't come any more?

I know she's not ready.

Not *yet*.

With my other hand I pinch one nipple, making her moan even louder, my fingers still working her clit as she fucks Lawson with abandon.

"I'm close," she whimpers, her head back and her eyes closed. Just those two words make my cock throb even harder, and I press myself against the firm globes of her ass, my lips against her neck.

"Come for us, peach," I growl, my voice bottoming out in my chest. "Stop holding back and come for us."

I pinch her nipple and clit just as Lawson pulls her down as hard as he can, and Jenna moans so loudly I'm sure we're going to get a noise complaint, her whole body trembling and shaking.

Then she comes, moaning Lawson's name and my name, all rolled into one, moving like a woman being rocked by a hurricane. Her head is back against my shoulder and she rolls her hips, Lawson's cock deep inside her as she comes.

I don't stop what I'm doing — my fingers on her nipple and clit — but I can feel it when Lawson comes inside her, his eyes rolling back into his head and his whole body going rigid.

I grab her breast in my hand, squeezing a little too hard, her delicate pink nipple between my fingers as Jenna sighs. I'm still massaging her clit with my other hand, working the swollen nub, and the sensations are jolting through her whole body with every pass my fingers make.

And she's moaning and whimpering, helpless little noises that I don't think she knows she's making, just saying *oh fuck, Lawson, Kade*, over and over again.

I can't take it anymore.

I run my fingers through Jenna's hair, make a loose fist, just enough to bring her head back but not enough to hurt her.

"My turn, peach," I whisper into her ear, and she moans again as I pull her upward, her hips unhinging as she kneels. Lawson's seed drips down the inside of her thigh, sticky and creamy, but I don't care. It's not like I've never seen the stuff before.

Jenna just bites her lip in response, a groan breaking through, and I push her forward until she's got her hand on Lawson's shoulders, on all fours over him. My cock is dripping with anticipation, so hard it aches.

My hand still in her hair, I grab her hips with my other hand, steadying my cock at her entrance. I can already feel how hot and slick she is, her back arched as she begs me with her body for *more*.

I breathe hard, fingers digging into her hip, but I take a moment and drag my hand over her back, over the twin globes of her ass, through the sticky mess around her pussy and to her clit, where she jolts with sensation yet again. Her pussy spasms around the head of my cock, like she's desperate for me to fuck her.

"You want more, don't you?" I growl.

I slide my tip against her heat, feeling her shiver beneath me.

"Yes," she moans. I pull on her hair lightly, just enough to feel another shudder of desire run through her body.

"Tell me," I say. "Beg me, peach. Say how badly you want to get fucked again, even though you just rode Lawson's cock good and hard."

She gasps, her breathing ragged.

"I want you—" she starts, then stops.

I can't help myself. I fucking love this about her, love how even though she's about to fuck both her bosses in the space of five minutes, how even though she's our sweet filthy peach and there's no part of her that's off-limits to us, she's still shy about saying it out loud.

"Tell me you want another thick cock deep inside you," I say, grabbing one ass cheek in my hand and squeezing. Her pussy spasms again, like she's trying to draw me in. "Tell me how you need a good fucking before you go to today's meeting and pretend to be a nice girl."

She inhales sharply, rocking back on her hands and knees like she's trying to get me inside her, but I don't let her do it, rocking back with her.

"I want you to fuck me," she says quickly, the words all coming out in a rush. "Oh God, Kade, I need you to fuck me hard and deep, *please.*"

Her sentence isn't even finished when I'm already plowing deep inside her slick, swollen pussy, bottoming out as her words turn into nothing but noises.

"Like that?" I hiss between my teeth, barely able to form words. She's still just as tight as the first time I fucked her, and she feels so good I have to pause for a moment just to get my bearings.

"Yes," Jenna whimpers, her pussy clenching around me with the words. She's so close to coming that I know nearly anything might send her over the edge, but I want to let her hover there, quivering on the precipice before I send her over.

"Good girl," I murmur, still not moving. My heart is thumping wildly, almost out of control, my breathing frantic.

We're still both straddling Lawson, who's utterly spent, and I can see him lift his hands. There's a sharp gasp from Jenna, and I know he's pinching her nipples from the way her back arches just a little more, the pleasured hitch in her breathing.

I relax my grip on her hair just enough for her lower her face to his, Lawson's fingers coming around her ribcage, pulling her in as he claims her mouth yet again and I watch. It's dirty, utterly filthy, but I love seeing my peach like this — with one cock hilt-deep in her pussy, while she makes out with the other man who just fucked her.

I love that's she's dirty, but more than that, I love that she's dirty for *us*.

Lawson's fingers find her clit again, and Jenna moans loudly, the sound muffled by his mouth as her pussy spasms and clenches again, her hips flexing and bucking. I swallow hard and slide out slowly, then fuck her again, making sure she can feel every millimeter of my thick cock as I enter her.

"Kade," she whimpers, her voice still muffled by Lawson. "Oh God, Kade."

Lawson's fingers on her clit move harder, faster, and Jenna trembles around me.

"Harder," she whispers.

My balls tighten, but I do it, fucking her deeper and harder than before, and she cries out with abandon, her tight body welcoming me as she does. I keep going, each stroke harder and faster than before, Lawson's fingers working her at the same time, until I'm certain I can't last any longer.

Jenna's got her head buried on Lawson's shoulder, moaning and whimpering.

"It feels so good," she groans, her voice desperate. "Oh my God, Kade, don't stop, don't ever stop—"

I stroke into her one last time, as hard and deep as I can, and I feel Jenna shatter around me. She cries out so loud she nearly screams, her voice muffled by the pillow and Lawson's shoulder, her pussy clenching my cock like a fist as she comes, her whole body writhing and jolting with pleasure.

I grab onto her hips, pushing myself deeper, and explode inside her like her body is begging me to. I come hard, my cock jerking again and again in time with her, until finally we're both completely spent.

After a long moment I pull out, my seed trickling out of her and down her inner thigh. I'm suddenly so exhausted I can barely move, but I flop down on the huge bed a few feet away from Lawson, leaving enough room for Jenna between us.

A moment later she's there, still breathing hard, and she looks up at me with her big eyes so I lean my face down and kiss her gently, one hand on her belly as I do. Lawson does the same a moment later, and then she's wrapped in our arms, safe and snug between us.

I know I have to go to work, go be a hardass in a room full of lawyers, but right now there's nowhere I'd rather be than here, with our peach, in this perfect afterglow.

After a long, long time, Jenna finally speaks up, her voice sleepy and sated.

"We should probably go to work, huh?" she says, laughing softly.

Lawson just kisses her head, and I chuckle quietly.

CHAPTER TWENTY-TWO

JENNA

THE REST OF THE TIME WE SPEND IN LONDON IS A WHIRLWIND. We're busy every single moment — working all day, with Lawson and Kade taking meetings and depositions, trying to untangle a tangled legal and financial web of shell companies, corporations and offshore accounts that I can't keep track of. It's a big case that they're on, one that'll take months, maybe years of eighty-hour weeks — but it's a case that could easily make them superstar attorneys once it's over.

And the nights? The moment that we're all done with work — even when it's at midnight — we always go back to either Kade or Lawson's hotel room and lose ourselves to pleasure. They do things to me I'd barely even dreamed of, dirty, *filthy* things that I never imagined I'd be doing with anyone.

Let alone two men at once.

Let alone my sexy, handsome, dominating bosses.

Kade eats me out with one finger in my ass, then two, touching pleasure centers that I didn't even know existed in my body. Lawson drapes me over a hotel room desk and fucks me hard while I swallow Kade's cock, my head dangling over the edge of the desk.

They take me into the shower, where Kade fucks me up against the wall while Lawson watches, and then Lawson takes his turn, bending me over while I brace my forearms against the slippery tile.

I come so many times that I lose count, the nights with them a haze of sinful pleasures, dirty talking and filthier acts that *should* feel wrong, but they don't.

With anyone else they might, but with Lawson and Kade there's a strange purity about them, just because I'm doing it with these two men — my firsts.

When we fly home, for once we're all too tired to do anything. I pass out the moment the plane takes off, in first class again, and don't wake up until our wheels hit the ground, even though I dream of that first plane ride.

The first day back in the office, I'm nervous. No — I'm nearly wrecked with anxiety, because before we all went to our respective homes last night, we didn't talk about anything. They simply paid for my taxi with their company credit card, kissed me goodnight, and left. We were all completely wiped out from the trip, between the jetlag and the total lack of sleep that we got while were in London.

When I walk in the front door of the office, I'm afraid of two things. One, that what we've done is somehow written on my face — that the moment everyone in the office looks at me, they'll somehow *know* that I spent the London trip getting fucked silly by my two bosses, that while I was there I lost my virginity to them and did things I'd never even considered before.

And two, I'm afraid that our affair was just that — an affair. That it was just a work trip fling, and now that we're home, it's suddenly over.

I don't want it to be over, because beyond the sex, beyond the endless pleasure — beyond the fact that I'll never be able to shower again without my pussy pulsing in anticipation — I think I'm falling for them.

Lawson and Kade are surprisingly sweet. Lawson knows exactly how to make Kade laugh; when it's the three of us alone, his charm becomes something more real. Something more like affection.

And as for Kade? Underneath that hard, spiky exterior he's sweet as sugar, a big, growly bear of a man who's taken to wrapping me in his muscled arms every night before he goes to sleep.

But when I get to work that next Monday, everything seems... *normal*. The receptionist at the front just gives me a single glance, then looks back at her computer screen; Brittany and Ashley, the other two secretaries in my corner of the office, just want to chat about what they did over the weekend. Sure, they ask politely about the London trip, but it's obvious that neither of them suspects anything — they just want to know what flying first class was like, and whether I got to do anything fun while I was there.

I tell them that it's great, and I didn't. We just worked the whole time.

The morning passes like everything is perfectly normal. I'm in before both Kade and Lawson, and when they walk in to their offices, they act like nothing's happened — they both just greet me, politely ask how I'm doing, then go into their respective offices and shut the doors.

I'm relieved. I'm mostly relieved.

But I'd be lying if I said I didn't secretly hope that something else would happen. It's been two days since I last saw them, a whole weekend — and they've been on my mind.

Was I secretly hoping that they'd come in this morning and ask to see me in an office, the door closed?

Was I secretly hoping that one of them would push my skirt up and pull me onto his lap, one hand in my hair, growling into my ear that I should be quiet if I don't want to alert everyone?

Was I secretly hoping that I'd find myself bent over the office desk, pussy exposed and blouse unbuttoned, as my bosses took turns with me?

Maybe I was hoping for all those things, just a little.

～

At 5:00 exactly, both Brittany and Ashley pack up their purses, switch off their computers, say goodnight, and head for the door. They're both career secretaries, women who have other ambitions in life besides working their way up the ladder.

Me? I'm not sure what I want career-wise — I wouldn't mind climbing a ladder, I just don't know which ladder I'd want to climb.

Slowly, the office empties out. By 5:15 nearly all the secretaries and assistants are gone, along with most of the attorneys — taking their work home with them, of course. My little corner of the open-plan office is nearly deserted, but I know that Lawson and Kade are still in their offices, slaving away over paperwork of some sort.

I'm not even hoping for an illicit rendezvous. I know that's insanely risky, and besides, I know better than anyone how busy these two are right now. I'm just hoping for... some kind of acknowledgement of what happened, and maybe — *maybe* — an invitation for it to happen again.

But by 5:20 I'm putting my things back into my purse. I sigh, turning off my computer, with one last glance at their office doors before I stand, slinging my purse over my shoulder.

I turn for the door and start trying to remember if I've got any food in the fridge. I think there's a leftover thing of fancy olives, maybe a bag of spinach, some milk if it hasn't gone bad yet, and of course I've always got dried pasta in the cabinet, at least if my roommate hasn't eaten it yet.

I could probably make something out of all that, I think. *It might not be good, but I won't starve.*

There might be some hummus, too, I wonder if I could incorporate that somehow....

"Jenna."

My heart skitters in my chest and I turn around instantly at the sound of Kade's voice. For an instant I feel like I'm in a vacuum, all the air sucked out of the room.

Then I turn around and try to act normal.

"Yes?" I ask, my stomach doing flip-flops inside me.

He doesn't answer right away, at least not with words. He's looking at me, desire in his burning gaze as he gives me a long, slow once-over, making my whole body tingle from the top of my head to the tips of my toes.

I go a little weak in the knees. I can't help it, because that single look promises everything I've been wanting all weekend — everything that they gave me again and again in London.

Everything that my vibrator was a *very* poor substitute for.

Finally, his eyes come back to mine, and I shiver involuntarily.

"Sorry, I can see you're just about to leave," he murmurs quietly, even though the office is nearly deserted. "Could we see you for just a moment? We need to discuss some things from our business trip."

My stomach clenches even harder, but at the mere words *business trip* all those memories come flooding back, the heat rocketing down my center. It's a ridiculous reaction, I know, but the mere thought of what we did has my panties already soaking wet.

"Of course," I say, hoping that I sound professional and not like someone who really wants to fuck her bosses again.

Kade turns, and I follow him past his own office and to Lawson's. A few people heading out for the day glance at us, but they barely notice us — after all, there's nothing unusual here.

Nothing unusual even when Kade lets me in first, then closes the door behind me, sparks of lightning flying up my spine.

Lawson's sitting there, behind his desk, wearing a charcoal gray suit. He leans back when I come in, one arm on an armrest, and a wide, charming smile lights up his handsome face.

"Sorry for corralling you on your way home," he says. "You couldn't spare us a moment, could you?"

I clear my throat and can't help but smile slightly, even as I can feel a blush creep up my neck to my cheeks.

"Of course I can," I say, my voice hushed, afraid that someone else still in the office will hear.

"Excellent," Kade says, stepping close behind me.

I'm positively quivering with desire, my heart hammering in my chest.

"Think you can be quiet?" he asks, his mouth now at my ear, Lawson watching with sharp eyes. There's a huge bulge in his pants already, and I feel like I can barely breathe.

"Yes," I whisper, my eyes already half-closed.

"Then lift your skirt and bend over the desk," Kade says, his hand already sliding up the back of my thigh, a small moan escaping my lips.

I obey him, and as I do, Lawson stands, shrugging off his suit jacket, his suit trousers nearly bursting at the zipper.

"Would you like to do some overtime?" he asks softly.

Over the next hour I come until I can barely stand, but to my credit, I don't make too much noise.

CHAPTER TWENTY-THREE

LAWSON

There are some things a lawyer shouldn't be.

Stupid, for one. A stupid lawyer doesn't do anyone any good.

Impatient, for another. My job involves hours, days, and even weeks of meticulously combing through boring documents, looking for the tiniest detail that could make or break a case.

Reckless, for a third.

Jenna makes me all three.

For the days and weeks following the trip to London, I'm all of those things. Every second that I'm not with her, I'm impatient until I am. I need Jenna like she's a drug, or like she's air or water. When I'm not with her I'm thinking about her, dreaming of the next time I can hear her laugh, watch her eyes light up.

I'm stupid. I can't stop watching her even when we're both on the clock, can't stop exchanging knowing glances with Kade across the office. I'm stupid enough to follow her into the supply closet, pretend I need a pencil, and then push her against the shelves and kiss her hungrily, pushing her skirt up to her waist.

I'm stupid enough to call her into my office, close the door, and then eat her out on my desk while Kade is there, hands down her shirt, mouth on hers.

I'm stupid enough to go home with the two of them every night for a couple of weeks, so stupid that I don't even bother to hide it — just drive away with her in the passenger seat of my Mercedes.

And all that stupidity and impatience makes me reckless. I know that we *can't* get caught, that it could cost all three of us our jobs — no matter that we're the top attorneys at our firm, they can't have this kind of scandal on their hands.

Reckless is both of us fucking Jenna in our offices, after hours. Reckless is the three of us going to the hotel down the block for a long lunch hour and coming back to five phone messages each and an office manager on the warpath, trying to figure out where Jenna went.

But I don't care, and neither does Kade. Neither of us gives even half a thought to that stuff, even though I know we *should.*

At the very least, we *should* go back to my high-rise condo before we take Jenna one after the other instead of bending her over a desk and making her moan our names. We *should* stop surprising her in a closed conference room and rubbing her quickly, through her panties, giving her a midday orgasm.

But we don't. It's like the mere sight of her shuts down our higher brain functions.

"You done yet?" Kade asks, leaning against the doorframe in my office. It's nearly seven, and almost everyone else has gone home — everyone except us and Jenna.

"Almost," I mutter. Between various meetings and other pointless bullshit, I've barely been able to work all day, almost until now — even though I found the time to get Jenna alone in a hallway and tell her what I'm going to do to her tonight.

I made her blush, which only made me want to do it more. I

love that about her, the way that she'll blush at dirty talk even if she's got a cock down her throat.

"We're ready whenever you are," he says, cocking one eyebrow.

Through the door, behind him, Jenna glances back at us, tucking a strand of strawberry-blonde hair behind one ear. I know we shouldn't be talking like this out in the open, even if the office is nearly empty, but again: she makes me stupid and reckless. I want her so much that I forget everything except *her*.

"All right," I mutter at Kade, even as my cock rises to half-mast at the mere thought of leaving the office and going home.

I was serious about what I told Jenna earlier, when I got her against the wall in a back hallway and whispered in her ear, the thing that made her blush so hard.

Tonight, we're taking your pretty little ass.

In my office, I exhale hard, blinking at the screen and the email I'm supposed to be writing. I force myself to focus on it for another thirty seconds, read it over once, and hit *send*.

"Okay," I say, shutting down my computer and rising from my chair.

"Good," Kade smirks. "It's about time."

Behind him, Jenna smiles shyly at me, then quickly blushes again. I know she's thinking about what I told her earlier, what Kade and I planned for her.

"Get your shit and let's go, then," I tell him, half-teasing. "Quit leaning in my doorway and move it."

Kade just chuckles and grabs his briefcase, his jacket slung over his arm. I quickly close and lock my office door behind myself, then walk out of the office and toward the elevator. My hand gravitates to Jenna's lower back because I can't help but touch her whenever we're together — even though I know how much trouble it could get me into.

While we wait for the elevator, I grab her ass quickly, give her squeeze.

"Lawson," she murmurs, like she's chiding me. Kade doesn't move, but one side of his mouth quirks up, like he's laughing at my impatience.

I squeeze her ass a little harder, bend my mouth to her ear.

"Forty-five minutes until I'm buried in your tight little ass, peach," I murmur.

The elevator doors open just as I finish my sentence, and I feel Jenna's whole body go rigid, but there's no one inside, and she relaxes again, and I can't help but chuckle as we board the elevator.

As the doors close, I slide my hand along her ass again, pushing my fingers between her legs to feel the heat there, even through the thick fabric of her pencil skirt. My hard-on is already raging.

Jenna turns around, her back now to the elevator doors, her mouth eagerly on mine. She cups my cock in her hand and I growl, instantly even harder—

"Hold the elevator!" a voice shouts from outside, the doors only a few inches apart.

Before I can do anything, an umbrella thrusts between them. They open, obligingly, revealing a sour-faced Marissa, and my heart drops into my stomach.

For a long moment, she just stands there, staring at me, umbrella still out, lips pursed like she's smelling a particularly nasty fart.

Oh, fuck.

Marissa's mouth settles into a thin line, taking it all in. She gives me a hard look, but then shifts her gaze to Jenna, glaring like she wants to set the girl on fire. I can already feel the heat creeping up Jenna's neck as all her muscles go rigid.

We got caught.

I can't fucking believe it. I got careless and now we're caught.

"Mind if I join you on the elevator to the parking garage?" Marissa asks acidly.

"Here, let me fix your earring," I say to Jenna, as my brain finally unfreezes and I think of an excuse, *any* excuse, for why I might be bending down like this.

She clears her throat once, then twice, swallowing hard.

"Thanks, that's better," she finally says.

I slide my hand from between her legs and step away, hoping Marissa didn't see, and gesture toward the buttons.

"Which floor?" I ask, trying to sound pleasant and genial, though God knows Marissa herself is never either of those things.

She just snorts, giving me a disgusted look.

"I've got it," she says, mashing the already-lit button for the parking garage before turning her back to us and staring at the elevator doors as if they need her personal attention to close properly.

Over Jenna's head, Kade shoots me a look. I shrug at him slightly.

Maybe Marissa bought it, I think, staring at her back. *I don't think she could see where my other hand was...*

When we reach the building's parking garage, Marissa gets off and walks away without even looking back at us.

"See you tomorrow," she calls out into the echoing concrete space.

It sounds like a threat, and I put my hand on Jenna's back as I feel her tense up again.

CHAPTER TWENTY-FOUR

KADE

"What the hell were you thinking?" I explode, the moment Lawson and Jenna open the door to my condo.

"Kade—" Lawson says, holding up both his hands, his tone placating.

"No," I growl at him as he shuts my front door, shrugging off his suit jacket. "We just got caught by *Marissa Fowler* of all fucking people, you can't just shrug that off. This is our jobs on the line, you *know* she'll go straight to—"

"She didn't see anything," Lawson says, his tone dismissive.

"The hell she didn't see anything," I say, pacing into my living room, throwing my own suit jacket over the back of my couch. "She jammed the doors open when you had one hand up Jenna's skirt and your tongue down her throat, because you can't wait *one second* until the doors were actually closed."

"So sue me," Lawson says.

I flop onto one of my overstuffed leather armchairs and *glare* at my best friend.

"You're not taking this seriously," I say in disbelief. "Marissa could easily go to Leonard with this. She could get you fired for sexual harassment, she could get Jenna fired for—"

"It wasn't sexual harassment," Jenna points out, walking into my living room as well.

"That's not how Leonard will see it," I say grimly.

She perches on the arm of my chair, and I notice she's got a button undone on her blouse, the lace of her white bra just barely peeking out. I clench my teeth and remind myself that I'm currently annoyed with her for putting all three of us at risk, but at the same time, I can't stop watching the rise and fall of her chest. I can't stop imagining putting my lips to her throat, sliding my fingers underneath that white lace until she gasps as I pinch her nipple.

"*Kade*," she says, like she's been trying to get my attention.

I look up at her face. She's tilting her head to one side, still perched on the arm of my chair. Across the room, Lawson walks over to my wet bar and pours himself a drink, glancing over his shoulder at us.

"I said I was sorry," Jenna tells me, amusement in her voice. "But Marissa's not as bad as you guys seem to think, she probably won't do anything."

Jenna cups my face in one hand, looking at me sweetly.

I glare at her, because it's working. She's distracting me from how annoyed I am at the two of them, making me want her even now, when they might have put all our jobs on the line.

"I promise not to do it again," she says, her hand trailing down my neck.

I swallow hard, try to retain my annoyance for a few more seconds.

"I'm just trying to keep my job," I growl. "And yours. And that jerk's, too," I say, nodding my head at Lawson across the room.

Jenna bites back a smile.

"We'll behave at the office from now on," she says, her eyes laughing.

"I wasn't the one who put a lunch meeting on the calendar so we could both eat her out midday," Lawson points out, drink in hand.

"We didn't get caught doing that, did we?" I ask.

"We could have," Jenna says.

I glance up at her, all that innocence and wickedness rolled into one package, and I can't take it anymore. I close my hand around her wrist and pull.

Jenna tumbles onto my lap, giggling, but her eyes go wide when I tighten my grip on her wrist and pull her against me so she's facing out, her back against my front.

"Is the problem that we're not satisfying you during non-work hours, peach?" I ask, my lips right against her ear.

My other hand finds her hip and pulls her down, my hard cock against her heat despite the layers of clothing separating us.

"Are you so unsatisfied that you can't wait three seconds until the elevator doors are closed?" I ask. "I thought we were doing pretty well by you, peach, but if you're going to need hourly orgasms during the workday, you can just say the word."

I slide my thumb underneath the hem of her pencil skirt, move it up her thigh. Across the room, Lawson gets a hungry look in his eye and starts walking toward me.

"No," I tell him. "Your punishment is that you only get to watch the first one."

"That's not much of a punishment," he says, smirking as he takes a sip.

I pull Jenna against my cock until she gasps and moans quietly, my hand skimming over her breast as I brush my knuckles against her damp panties. A shudder runs through her body at the sensation, and she leans back against me, rolling her hips.

"What do you think, peach?" I murmur into her ear, stroking her through the thin cloth of her underwear. "Shall we torture Lawson a little until he learns his lesson?"

I pinch her clit through her underwear and Jenna doesn't answer, just moans in response as she bucks her hips against me, her knees going wide. The movement hikes her skirt up to her waist and now I can smell her arousal, clear as day.

Dear God, I want her. Having to see her twenty times a day while I work is pure torture, because if I had my way, I'd schedule a lunch meeting to eat her pussy every single day. Half the time when I sit in meetings with clients all I can think about is the way she cries our names out when she comes, or the way she sometimes smiles when she falls asleep.

I keep stroking her through her panties, listening to the way her breathing sharpens, feeing the way her body goes rigid and then soft with each movement of my fingers.

"Unbutton your blouse," I murmur into her ear. "Slowly."

Her breathing hitches, but her hands come up. Over her shoulder I'm watching Lawson, still sitting in the chair opposite us, his drink all but forgotten in his hand. His eyes are burning with lust, and I can track how many buttons Jenna's undone by how his gaze drops.

Jenna shrugs her blouse off, then tosses it next to the chair, unconsciously straightening one white lacy bra strap, then glancing over her shoulder at me, across the room to Lawson.

I hook my finger under her bra strap and pull it over her shoulder, my other hand still working her through her wet panties. Jenna makes a noise, deep in her throat, and I bite her shoulder just hard enough that she can feel it.

Lawson hasn't moved this whole time.

"You like it when you've got an audience, don't you?" I murmur into her ear. She writhes against me again in response.

I stop rubbing her for a moment, hook my thumbs under her skirt, and pull it down and off while she's still on my lap. Now all she's wearing is matching white lace panties and a bra, the very picture of disheveled, naughty innocence.

Fuck, I love this.

"Since you two nearly got us all fired, don't you think it's fair that I decide what's next?" I ask her, fingers dipping below her panties. Lawson's eyes are on them, and even though his posture is perfectly casual, I can see his huge, painful erection.

Good. I want him to suffer for his stupidity, at least a little. He doesn't say anything in response, and Jenna just moans as I stroke her a little harder, a little faster, my fingers sliding through her slick wetness.

With my other hand I undo her bra, toss it aside, take one breast in my hand and pinch her nipple until she gasps, her head forward, hair tumbling over her face as she grinds herself against my rock-hard cock. Lawson can't stop watching her, gripping his glass so hard I think he might break it.

"Good," I say, even though no one answered me. "Because I'm going to fuck you while he watches, and I'm not going to let you come until I think you've learned your lesson."

Jenna whimpers once, leaning forward, one hand on my knee. She rolls her hips slowly over my achingly hard length, so wet that there's a damp spot on my suit pants.

Lawson growls, but he doesn't move.

I push Jenna forward slightly, undo my pants, finally free my cock. I can't help but sigh with relief, groaning as I pump myself once. Jenna looks back at me over her shoulder, biting her lip.

Then, out of nowhere, I have the urge to kiss her. In this moment she's so raw, so vulnerable, so *beautiful* that I just want to kiss her.

So I do. I kiss the hell out of Jenna, pulling her backward, her nearly-naked body against my fully clothed one, my best friend and her lover still watching from his chair. It's a long, slow kiss, my hands wandering her slim body.

Finally, they're at the waist of her pretty lace panties, and suddenly, I can't wait any longer. I grab them in both hands and pull in opposite directions, the material tearing in my strong hands. Jenna gasps and moans, and I pull away from our kiss, tossing her torn panties on the floor.

"Don't worry, I'll buy you a new pair," I growl in her ear.

CHAPTER TWENTY-FIVE

JENNA

I THINK I'M MELTING.

If Kade wanted to torture me for being too impatient and kissing Lawson before the elevator door shut, he's doing a great job of it, because I feel like I'm losing my mind.

From one direction, there's Kade — hands everywhere, teasing me, telling me the things he's about to do to me. I'm silently begging him to do them, because I can't help but grind against his thick cock, desperately wanting to feel his hard length inside me.

In the other direction is Lawson, his eyes burning with lust, desire and — maybe — *jealousy*. I've never felt that before between these two, but there's something taut and dangerous in the air right now, something that feels like it could snap at any moment.

"Do I have to beg?" I whisper to Kade, surprised at the sound of my own voice.

He chuckles, grabbing my shoulder and pushing me forward. I steady myself with my hands on his knees, holding my head up, looking Lawson right in the eyes.

I don't think I'll ever get enough of the way he's looking at me right now, the unbridled lust and passion in his gaze.

Then Kade's hand is on my hip, pulling me back, the tip of his cock just grazing along my entrance.

"Please," I moan, unable to stop myself. My fingers tighten on his knee, and I roll my hips back, desperate to have him inside me. "Kade, *please.*"

He doesn't respond, but all at once he's got both hands on my hips and he pulls me back. I take his entire hard, thick length in one stroke and he hits every pleasure center in my body as he hilts himself deep, stretching me and filling me and feeling even better than I'd dared to imagine.

Before I know it I'm sitting fully upright, one of his hands knotted in my hair, straddling his legs, his cock still deep inside me. He's still wearing his suit and I'm completely naked, completely vulnerable.

Someone's moaning. It must be me, because I'm fully on display to Lawson, legs wide, sitting up as I take Kade's cock.

"This what you wanted when you decided to make out with him in the elevator?" Kade asks, but his voice has a softer edge to it. "When you couldn't wait to have a cock inside you, so you nearly got us all fired?"

My eyes at half-mast, vision blurred with pleasure, I look up at Lawson. He's on the edge of his seat, still looking ready to devour me.

"Yes," I moan.

I try to move because the one driving force in my body right now is to ride Kade's thick cock as hard as I can. I want him slamming into me, taking me hard and deep while Lawson watches. I *need* him to make me lose all control and fly to pieces, but instead he holds me down by the hips, his cock pulsing inside me.

He just chuckles.

"I don't think so," he says, his voice gravelly and sweet all at once. "If I give you what you want now, you'll just do it again. Instead I'm going to teach both of you a lesson."

With that, he starts moving slowly, his cock barely shifting inside me just enough to hit all my pleasure centers. I'm stuffed so full that I can feel every millimeter he moves, my pussy stretching around him.

Kade snakes one hand around me, and suddenly his fingers are on my wet clit, stroking and rubbing and circling in perfect time with his cock. I'm half leaning forward, my hands still on his knees, and I dig my nails into his legs at the sudden pleasure.

"Your cock feels so good," I moan, totally unable to control myself. "You're gonna make me come so fast."

Behind me, his breathing hitches but his hand slows on my clit, and suddenly I'm no longer near that edge.

"No, I'm not," he says, a smirk in his voice.

I try to make him move harder, faster, to fuck him like I *want* to but I'm not in control here. *He* is, and he wants to torture me.

Kade doesn't pick up the pace. He keeps it up, barely moving, pushing me toward the edge again and again with his cock and his hand but never sending me over, until I feel like my body is made up of shimmering lava, pure heat pounding through my veins.

"Make me come," I hear myself begging him. "Please, Kade, *please*. I need to come, your cock feels so good inside me, *please*."

There's a hand on my nipple, pinching one and then the other almost to the point of pain. Then the hand is back on my clit, circling and rubbing, then stilling. I moan and it comes out as a whimper, my hands and toes curled. I'm willing myself to come with every single muscle in my body, but I can't.

I'm right there, on the edge, but I can't yet.

"Have you learned your lesson, peach?" he asks softly, sliding two fingers around my clit, holding it tight.

"Don't fuck at work," I gasp, leaning forward, into his touch. I roll my hips, try to draw him even deeper, but it doesn't work.

"Don't fuck where you can get caught," he says, his voice a purr. "I very much like fucking at work."

Suddenly he pulls me onto him *hard*, his fingers rubbing me furiously as Kade finally fucks me hard and fast and mercilessly.

I come instantly, all the pent-up energy exploding out of me in a long, loud moan that's probably so loud they can hear it in Brooklyn. I'm hot and cold at the same time, the sensation so intense that it feels like being showered by snow and sparks all at once.

When I open my eyes, Lawson is standing in front of me, his hands on my face, and he's looking down at me with an intensity I've never seen before.

Even as the aftershocks of the orgasm run through my body, he traces his thumb along my lower lip.

"You're so fucking beautiful," he murmurs quietly, his eyes boring down into mine. "Especially when you come."

My eyes land on his massive erection, straining so hard against his zipper that it's stretching the material of his suit. I bite my lower lip in my teeth and take his thick length in my hand, stroking him through his pants as he kisses me deeply, his tongue invading my mouth.

I feel taken. Possessed. *Owned*, by these two powerful, sexy men, one kissing me like his life depends on it and the other still hard inside me. Part of me wonders if I should feel used, dirty, like a whore, but I don't.

There's something magical about this moment, something pure and beautiful despite the raw sexuality. Like this is who I'm *supposed* to be with.

Most people don't find their perfect match ever. Is it possible that I found two?

After a long, slow kiss, Lawson pulls back. He runs his thumb over my lips again, then smiles at me, wickedness gleaming in his eyes.

"Now," he says softly. "What did I promise you earlier?"

Lawson doesn't wait for an answer. He lifts me off of Kade so I wrap my legs around him, kissing me deeply again. I gasp at the void inside me, but before I know it he's spun around, set me down on the leather couch as he takes off his suit jacket, then his shirt.

I swallow hard. Even though I see him all the time, even though Kade was just inside me, Lawson's body always takes my breath away. He's got sculpted, chiseled muscles, and watching them stretch and pull as he takes off his shirt and undoes his belt makes heat pool in my belly all over again.

He takes his pants off, his huge cock springing out as he kicks them away and leans forward again. I take him in one hand, moaning softly as I give him a long, hard stroke from root to tip.

Lawson kisses me again, and behind him, I'm vaguely aware that Kade is standing from his chair, taking his own suit off, but then Lawson pulls back, my lower lip between his teeth.

"Remind me what I said I was going to do to you," he says, his voice low and teasing.

My insides squirm, half in wild anticipation and half in sudden anxiety, the thought of his lips against my ear as he whispered *I'm going to fuck your ass* shuddering through me.

"You don't remember?" I ask him, one hand on his chest, suddenly coy.

Lawson laughs and kisses my fingers, but the ferocity in his eyes doesn't go anywhere.

"I want you to say it," he says, his eyes burning into mine as he lowers his voice. "I want you to ask me for it, peach."

I swallow hard, my mouth suddenly dry, my stomach doing somersaults inside me. I don't know why *this* of all things suddenly feels so dirty, but it does.

"You're going to…" I whisper, voice trailing off.

Just say it, Jenna, I tell myself.

"Fuck my ass," I finish.

The smile that spreads slowly over Lawson's face is unlike anything I've seen before — it's hungry and lusty and loving all at once, his eyes roaming over my body like it belongs to him.

"Good girl," he murmurs.

I lean up for the kiss that I think is coming, but instead Lawson suddenly scoops me up and before I know it I'm facing the other direction, bent over, forearms resting on the back of the couch where Kade's standing.

I didn't even see him go back there, but he puts one finger under my chin and tilts it up, giving me a slow, hard kiss that leaves me breathless.

"I love watching him fuck you," Kade breathes into my ear. "Almost as much as I love fucking you myself."

With that, the tip of Lawson's cock slides along me, starting at my slick entrance, moving to the sensitive nub of my clit, and then back down. I swallow hard and try to relax, but I can't help tensing up, my hands forming fists as I force myself to breathe.

But instead, suddenly, Lawson's sliding into my pussy, stretching me as I grip him, and I moan out loud, face still in Kade's hands. My eyes slide shut with the unexpected pleasure, and involuntarily I tighten as his thick cock hits all my pleasure centers in a row as he fucks me slow and hard.

Behind me, he chuckles. There's the sound of a bottle opening, and then then something liquid and slippery on my other hole, followed by Lawson's gentle, probing finger.

"I'm not a barbarian, peach," he teases me. "I'm a gentleman and I'm going to fuck your ass like one."

He slides one finger into my tight back hole, and my vision goes blurry with the sudden added pleasure, his cock still filling my pussy. I moan again, and Kade kisses me deeply, his tongue exploring my mouth as he does. He's naked too, now, his still-hard cock bobbing in front of me.

Lawson adds a second finger, then a third, as he fucks me slowly with both his hand and his cock. This isn't the first time that one of them has put their fingers in my ass — not even the first time they've done it while fucking me — but it's the first time they've filled me up this much, the first time that I feel like I can barely function from the sheer pleasure.

"Lawson," I gasp. "More."

He just chuckles, his breathing heavy as he fucks me gently.

"Soon," he says, his voice a growl.

Kade's thumb is in my mouth, somehow, and I suck on it greedily, my tongue swiping over the salty rough pad. I'm moaning constantly now, the pure pleasure of being double-fucked almost too much for me.

Slowly, the wave breaks over me, and I come still moaning, Kade's thumb in my mouth as I suck it harder and harder. My body shudders and I can feel my pussy clamping down around Lawson's thick, still-hard cock, stretching me and using me together with his fingers.

I shouldn't like it, but I do. I shouldn't be here, and I definitely shouldn't be doing *this*, but I am. I've fucked two men — my *bosses*, no less — in the space of just a few minutes, and now Lawson is slowly pulling his cock and fingers out of me as the aftershocks rock through my body.

I look up at Kade, meet his lust-dark eyes, and I can only think one thing.

"Fuck my ass," I whisper, voice shaking slightly. "Please."

There's more of the slippery liquid on my back hole, but then the tip of Lawson's cock is there, pressing gently in. He widens me gradually, taking his time, and I can feel myself stretching to accommodate his girth.

"Relax," Kade says, running his thumb over my bottom lip again, watching us hungrily. "Just relax and let him fuck you."

Kade's cock is bobbing in front of me, and I can see the

pearlescent precum dripping steadily from the engorged tip as Lawson slides deeper and deeper with every tiny thrust.

I take a deep breath. I make myself relax, even though my body is still shaking with the new sensations taking place as he stretches me to fit him.

It feels so strange and wonderful all at once, like there's no possible way that this could work but at the same time I want this *desperately*, I want to feel pleasures I've never felt before and I want to give him — them — this gift.

I want my body to be *theirs*. I want them to use me however they want, in every hole, in every way.

And it doesn't hurt, not quite, but with every shallow stroke Lawson stretches me a little wider, wider than I thought I could possibly go. I'm moaning with the sheer force of wanting him inside me, pushing back against him just a little.

Suddenly, just when I think I can't possibly take anymore, there's a tiny popping sensation, and then Lawson stops. I'm gasping for breath, back hole spread wide, and he smooths his hands over the expanse of my back before he bends and kisses the back of my neck.

"The hard part's over," he whispers roughly.

"Lawson," I moan. "It feels—"

My words break off into a long groan of pleasure as he rocks deeper into me. I feel like he's splitting me in half with his cock, only instead of pain, it feels incredible.

"Please," I whisper, even though I don't know what I'm asking him for.

"You're so fucking tight," he growls in my ear, his hands sliding over my breasts, tweaking my stiff nipples.

My eyes flutter closed as Lawson moves deeper inside me. I can barely breathe, let alone think — he's hitting pleasure centers that I'd never dreamed existed, touching nerves I didn't know I had. It's so much dirtier than I ever thought I'd be, but I can't help it.

I love getting fucked in the ass by my boss.

His cock pushes deeper and deeper into me. I'm moaning and whimpering with wild abandon, and even though I barely notice, Kade's hand is on my face, caressing my lower lip, his fingers sliding through my hair and taking hold.

Suddenly, I feel Lawson's hips flush against my ass, and I groan even louder as he hilts himself deep in me.

"You like having your tight little ass filled with cock?" he asks. "Does it feel good when I stretch you out, peach?"

I can barely talk, but I manage to gasp out, "Yes."

"Good," he grunts.

Lawson pulls his cock back, almost all the way out, and I moan again. Suddenly Kade's cock is there, in front of my face, and for a moment I wonder how long it's been there.

Then I stop thinking, reach out, and take it in my hand.

"That's right, peach," Kade murmurs as I give him a long hard stroke, my juices still slick on his shaft.

Lawson fills me again, harder this time, and I moan as my vision begins to sparkle white. I had no idea this could feel so dirty and so *good*, all at once.

Kade's cock is still bobbing in front of my face, and as Lawson keeps fucking my ass, I open my mouth and swallow Kade. I've learned to deep throat them in a single stroke, totally suppressing my gag reflex, and over the sounds of Lawson's groans I can hear the hitch in Kade's breath when I do.

It's almost too much to have them both inside me like this, sharing me. It feels so good I almost can't bear it, as the wave of pleasure coursing through my body crests again and again.

Lawson fucks me harder, faster, and now Kade's hand is in my hair, pulling my head back. I swallow him again and again, licking and sucking as he pulls out with each stroke while they move in a perfect rhythm and I moan nonstop.

"God, you're beautiful with my cock in your mouth," Kade

grunts, his shaft disappearing between my lips. I take him, push him deep, savor the way he groans when I do.

"The only thing I like better than watching you suck my cock is watching you suck my cock while he fucks you in the ass," he goes on.

I whimper with pleasure just as another wave crests. These two men have somehow flipped a switch inside me, sensitizing my whole body. I couldn't stop coming, even if I wanted to.

"I'm gonna come, peach," Lawson groans. His fingers dig into my shoulder, probably leaving bruises, as he fills me as hard and deep as he can. I moan around Kade's cock, even as I suck his juices off.

"Please," I whisper. "Come inside me, Lawson."

He slams into me one last time and I come yet again, my whole body shaking and shuddering with the force of the orgasm, even as I open my mouth and suck Kade down again, savoring the taste of his girth.

I come so hard I'm afraid I'll pass out, but then I realize Lawson is leaning over me, cock in my ass, groaning and murmuring in my ear.

"So fucking good, peach, *so* fucking good..."

Suddenly Kade's cock jerks in my mouth and I swallow him again, taking him down the tight shaft of my throat just as he comes in long, thick spurts, his fingers tight in my hair. I swallow again and again, savoring the feel of both of them coming inside me at once.

After a moment, Kade pulls out. Without missing a beat, he grabs a tissue from a side table and wipes my face off tenderly, finally planting a soft, slow kiss on my lips when he's done.

Moments later, Lawson pulls out as well and before I can move, he's wrapped me tight in his strong arms, lifting me. I can barely move, I'm so exhausted, but in a good way.

Lawson carries me to the shower, where he and Kade take turns washing me off so tenderly and gently I can barely believe it. They even wash and condition my hair without me having to ask, and when they're done, they lift me onto the huge king-sized bed and take turns eating me out.

When they're both done, I drift off to sleep wedged between them, as blissfully happy as I've ever been.

CHAPTER TWENTY-SIX

LAWSON

AFTER THE INCIDENT IN THE ELEVATOR, I KNOW WE HAVE TO BE more careful, as hard as it is. I see the narrow-eyed look that Marissa gives me in the office the day after, and even though I give her the same charming smile as ever, I know it's a warning.

I know what she saw, even if I can tell she's not quite sure. After all, we would have to be *absolutely crazy* to do something like that with an employee.

Let alone at the office.

Let alone where we could be caught.

But that's the problem: I'm absolutely crazy about Jenna, and I can barely help myself around her.

For a few days we behave ourselves properly. Even though I have to see her almost all day, and even though it drives me up the wall, I don't push her tight skirt up and taste her the way I want to. I don't call her into my office so I can bend her over the desk and take her hard, the way I want to.

Instead, I'm reduced to jerking off in a bathroom stall. One day, an extra button on her shirt comes unbuttoned for a few minutes and I can see the tiniest bit of lace froth through the top.

That day, I jerk off twice in the bathroom.

This is what she reduces me to.

A week goes by like that, and I convince myself that we'll be fine. I know that Kade is every bit as frustrated as I am, even though I also know that we both worked here for *years* and didn't have sex at the office once.

I never even wanted to, before Jenna.

It's only since having her that *not* doing it has become nearly unbearable.

DOCUMENT REVIEW TURNS out to be our downfall. We're shut in a small conference room for hours and hours, just the three of us, and I feel like my nerve endings are peeling away from my body with desperation. Jenna's wearing a white blouse — buttoned high, this time — and a gray pencil skirt with heels.

There *shouldn't* be anything tempting or salacious about her outfit. There are probably five other women in the office wearing nearly the exact same thing, and I didn't look at any of them twice.

But on Jenna, I can't stand it. By six o'clock that night I've had a hard-on for most of the day and I can't focus on the sheets of paper in front of me.

I know that Kade is feeling the same thing, our ties loosened, our jackets tossed over chairs.

Finally, Jenna looks up at me once, tapping her pen on her lower lip. I see her eyes dip to my lap just once before she recovers, but the look of hunger is unmistakable in them.

"We're only halfway through the financials," she says. "We could keep going and finish tonight, or—"

Kade stands without saying anything and locks the door.

Fuck.

Without missing a beat, he takes off his tie and practically dives under the table. Jenna grabs the edge of it hard, that unmistakable hitch in her breathing as her eyes go wide.

Seconds later I hear Kade's groan of satisfaction as Jenna slouches in her chair, her eyes losing focus as she presses her lips together, trying to keep herself from moaning as Kade eats her out under the table.

I can't stop myself anymore. There's no point in trying, and in seconds I'm across the table, capturing Jenna's mouth with my own, both hands down her shirt as she gasps into my mouth.

Ten minutes later, she's riding Kade's cock in one of the office chairs while she sucks me off, and I just have to pray that her quiet-but-enthusiastic moans can't be heard beyond the door.

AFTER THAT EVENING in the conference room, it's like the floodgates open, and all the effort I put into behaving myself at work is utterly undone. The next evening, still doing document review, we take turns bending her over the conference table and fucking her fast and hard until we all come, Jenna hardest of all.

We can't always be together, so Kade and I take turns. With anyone else I'd be insanely jealous, possessive, *furious*. But with Kade, all I can think about is how fucking sexy Jenna looks when she's gripped by desire, the way her mouth opens just a little bit when she comes.

I follow her into the women's restroom, lock the door, and eat her out on the sinks. Kade gets a blowjob while he's on a long, boring conference call. I eat her out with one finger in her ass during my lunch hour one day.

I fuck her hard and slow in the supply closet. Kade does, too.

She's still coming home with us every night, and every night, we're still falling asleep all tangled together, Jenna in between us. Then, when we wake up, we each take separate cars to work and act like we've been apart.

It's like nothing I've ever felt before. Even when we go to work separately in the morning — trying to keep up the facade — I miss her for the twenty minutes we spend apart. When I see her again at the office, my heart sings and I know there's a stupid smile on my face.

Kade's too.

I think we're both in love with our legal assistant.

And I have no idea what happens next.

JENNA WHIMPERS, her voice soft and muffled. I've got one hand over her mouth because I know she can't help but make noise sometimes, and her pussy clenches relentlessly around me, her back arching as her body bucks.

"Shh, you dirty thing," I whisper in her ear. "Unless you *want* to get caught taking me balls-deep in the law library."

She gasps again, and I start moving inside her, just barely budging up against her pleasure spots. Her tight channel is still fluttering around me, and I take a moment to collect myself.

I *should* just let myself finish and get back to work. Right now Jenna is braced against the back shelf of our law library, face-to-face with row after row of blue-bound law books. She's already come twice, but I love being inside her so much that I want just *one* more.

What can I say? I'm selfish.

I start to move again, harder and faster, when suddenly she tries to say something. I take my hand off of her mouth, and she looks up at me, eyes heavy-lidded with desire.

"Harder?" I murmur in her ear.

She shakes her head, and I swear she's blushing.

"Fuck me in the ass," she whispers, her eyes pleading.

I stop for a moment and swallow hard, a slow grin spreading across my face.

"Here?" I murmur, licking the outer shell of her ear. "Now, you dirty girl?"

"Please," she whispers, leaning forward, her hand already on the base of my cock as it slides out of her.

I'm throbbing, desire pounding through my cock at what she just suggested. There's been no shortage of anal since the first night I fucked Jenna in the ass — it turns out that our sweet, dirty girl *loves* it.

But here? At work? Where anyone could walk in and find us?

God, it's hot, but it's dangerous. I swallow hard again, balls clenching.

"I don't have any lube," I tell her. It's not like I was expecting this.

"It's okay," she murmurs back. "Lawson, I'm so wet, you're already soaked…"

I reach my hand down to her swollen, slippery pussy. She's right, of course. I take her juices on my fingers and slowly, tenderly slide them over her back hole, her hand already tight on my cock.

Jenna bites her lip, stifling another moan.

Then, before I can dip a finger into her ass to prepare her, she's guiding my cock to her tight entrance, pushing her hips back, her mouth open in an O of pleasure.

"Please," she says again, the thick head of my cock sliding into her. "Please, Lawson, I need you—"

Her words turn into a quiet moan as the head of my cock pushes past that ring of muscle. I quickly cover her mouth with my other hand as white-hot pleasure washes over me with her tightness.

"Is this what you wanted?" I hiss in her ear as I hilt myself deep, a tremor running through her body. "You get dirtier every day, peach, and I fucking love it. Maybe tomorrow we'll come in here and take turns fucking your tight little ass."

Jenna can't speak, but her eyes roll back into her head and I feel her start to come, her passage clenching rhythmically around my cock. I push her even harder up against the law books and fuck her hard and fast, utterly unable to stop myself as I pound Jenna furiously, right there at work.

She comes hard, again and again, the only sound her quiet whimpers from behind my hand as she begs me not to stop.

Finally, I plow her deep one last time and spill myself inside her with a groan that I can't stop, holding her tight against my chest as I pulse again and again, coming so hard I can barely stay on my feet.

I feel a little guilty that Kade wasn't here, but I'm one hundred percent sure he'll get his chance to fuck Jenna's ass in the law library before much longer.

The girl is *insatiable*. I love that about her.

Just as I'm about to pull out, kissing her on the side of her head, I hear a sound.

The unmistakable *click* of a door closing. My heart freezes, and I duck my head, scanning the library between rows of books, pulse thumping through my veins.

What the fuck was I thinking?

What's wrong with you? You couldn't wait six hours?

"Who is it?" Jenna whispers, voice tremulous.

"I don't know," I whisper back. "I don't see anyone."

There's no one there. The room that houses our law library isn't that big, and unless someone is on the floor, I'd be able to see them.

She looks at me with wide, nervous eyes, biting her lip gently with her teeth. I kiss her softly, a reassuring hand on her shoulder.

"I'm sure it was nothing," I murmur.

CHAPTER TWENTY-SEVEN

KADE

I'M PRETTY SURE THAT LAWSON AND JENNA ARE TOGETHER somewhere right now. I'm almost certain they're fucking — maybe in the supply closet again, maybe in the law library this time — and I can't concentrate on what I'm doing in the least.

I wish I were there, even though I know that would be too suspicious. One lawyer missing for twenty minutes is no big deal, but two? Along with their assistant?

Then people would start searching for us, and that's the last thing I want.

But dear God, thinking about what they're doing right now is getting me hard as a rock, even though I'm sitting at my desk, trying to read through this deposition about tedious tax law.

Is he eating her out? Is she up on a desk, or maybe on the floor, or standing bent over as he licks her sweet pussy again and again until she cries out and her legs shake?

Or is he fucking her, getting to watch the glorious way that the pink flush spreads from her chest to her neck as she comes?

Maybe tonight's the night, I think.

Then I shake my head quickly, banishing the thought.

Jenna's not ready. She was a virgin two weeks ago, there's no way she can take us both at once...

Something pops up on my computer screen, but I ignore it completely. Instead I'm imagining the three of us. On my bed, in my condo, Jenna already riding Lawson, her cries of pleasure echoing off the walls.

The sweet moment when I come up behind her and she leans forward, looking at me through her lashes over her shoulder.

The way it'll feel when I take her in her back hole with him already inside her pussy, tighter than I could possibly imagine.

How hard Jenna will come *then*, the way pleasure's going to take her body over completely.

My computer beeps again and I shake my head, forcing myself back to the reality of this deposition. I'm already stroking myself through my suit pants, my big mahogany desk hiding my erection, and for a split second I consider closing my office door and jerking off.

What the hell is wrong with you? I ask myself.

Back to the task at hand. Or *not* at hand, as the case may be.

TEN MINUTES LATER, Marissa storms through the office. I'm not really paying attention — I'm still trying to wrangle these documents — but I've got my office door partly open, so I watch her blast by everyone in there and head into Paul Leonard's office without even knocking.

That gets my attention. Doing that is unimaginable even for me, and I'm a full partner at the law firm. Hell, I once watched Paul Leonard make a forty-year-old man cry for interrupting a phone call.

But it also gets my attention that Lawson and Jenna are nowhere to be seen. Maybe they weren't doing anything —

maybe Lawson needed her for a meeting, or he's grabbing a late lunch while she un-jams the printer in the other room.

I've nearly convinced myself of that when I finally see them. Jenna's first, walking out of the hallway and toward her desk, and she's got the faintest blush on her cheeks, the rosy glow that tells me she just came hard somewhere else. Right before she sits at her desk she flicks her gaze to me for just a moment, then looks away, an unmistakable smile in her eyes.

A few minutes later Lawson walks the same way. Even though he's immaculately put together as always, not a single wrinkle in his suit, I can tell what he just did. We've been best friends for years. We've fucked a dozen women together. I know what's going on, and the heat in my core builds just *thinking* about it.

It's nearly five o'clock. I don't have anything today that will mandate overtime, so as soon as the clock strikes the hour, I'm out of here. We'll go to my place tonight, and the second I get in the door I'm going to pick up Jenna, take her to a chair, and sit her right on my—

"Mr. Chandler?" a knock on my door pushes me out of my reverie, and I look up to see Linda, Paul's executive assistant. She's as no-nonsense as they come, with a helmet of brown hair and half-moon spectacles that reside on a chain around her neck.

"Yes?"

"Mr. Leonard wants to see you in his office," she says, her voice perfectly neutral.

Even so, it feels like a cold knife into my gut. If he knows, I could lose my job — and worse, for something like this, I'm sure I'll be blacklisted from every firm in New York City.

All because of a girl.

"Of course," I say. "Is this about the DiMaggio case?"

Her eyebrows lift slightly, and *those* hopes are crushed.

"I don't believe so," she tells me, with a perfectly neutral tone that tells me she knows *exactly* what this is about, and it's not going to be good for me.

I stand without answering her and grab my suit jacket on the way out the door, following Linda through the busy office and to Paul's door. I can feel eyes on us, but I ignore them.

"Sit," Paul says the moment I get into his office. I sink into one of three rich leather chairs arrayed in front of his desk.

He doesn't even look at me, totally focused on the computer screen in front of him. A moment later, Jenna steps through the door, followed by Lawson.

This isn't good. Jenna looks terrified, like she might cry, and Lawson looks pissed and more than a little protective. Seeing her like this riles up something fierce deep inside me, and I sit forward, ready to defend my woman at all costs.

"Do you know how long Hamilton, Clark, and Leonard has been in business?" he asks, his voice brusque.

"No," I say, together in chorus with Lawson.

Poor Jenna looks too terrified to even open her mouth.

"Fifty-three years," he says, answering his own question. "We have been a pillar of the community for fifty-three years, and you know how we did that?"

I don't bother answering this time as he hits his palm against his desk.

"Integrity. Charity. Moral uprightness."

Defending rich people against accusations of tax fraud, I think.

"And absolutely *no* hanky-panky."

Here he stops and glares at each of the three of us in turn. I glare back, resisting the urge to reach out to Jenna and pull her into my arms.

Just get through this, I think. *Apologize, say it won't happen again, and get back to work.*

"Now," he says imperiously, both hands flat on his desk as he glares. "I'm *quite certain* that the incoming reports of *hanky-panky* are much overstated. I'm absolutely certain that the three of you know better than to, and I quote, 'get it on' in the lavatory in your workplace."

I glance at Jenna. She's bright red, red as a tomato, and a single tear tracks its way down her cheek. I have to grip my hands together in my lap to keep still.

I don't care that I'm being chastised. I don't even care that I'm being mocked. But her?

Fuck no.

"Of course not," Lawson murmurs, always better than me at controlling the outward display of his emotions.

"Good," Paul says. "Because I'd hate to think that the rumors of sexual intercourse in the law library were true, and I'd hate to think that one of my legal assistants was seeing *two* of my lawyers at once. Though, it does seem that you're aware of each other?"

He lifts his eyebrows expectantly. Neither of us answers.

"Well, that's good, I suppose, if a bit unorthodox. That said, of course you'll be terminating this relationship forthwith, as our employee handbook *clearly* states—"

"We won't," someone says, his voice hard as steel.

Then there's a pause. After a second, I realize who spoke.

It was me.

"Pardon?" Paul asks.

I clear my throat, not at all sure what I'm about to say. That was a knee-jerk reaction, an instinctive response to anyone suggesting I might give up Jenna.

"We're not ending this relationship," I say. "Fuck the employee handbook."

His eyebrows shoot almost to his hairline.

"Then I'll have no choice but to terminate you, but surely that's—"

"All right," Lawson says, standing.

Paul is baffled.

"Hold on, hold on," he says, gesturing with his palms out.

"This is insanity. You've been here for a few years, you're climbing the ladder steadily, you've both just made partner, you can't just throw it all away like this!"

I stand as well, my eyes on Jenna. She looks startled, shocked. I put one hand on her shoulder.

"I love you," I say softly. "And if this prick wants to fire me over that, it's fine with me."

"Kade," Jenna whispers softly. "That's crazy—"

"Well, it's exactly what we're going to do," Lawson says, on Jenna's other side. He kneels down next to her, taking her face in his hands. "We love you, Jenna, and nothing else matters."

Paul is still standing behind his desk, goggle-eyed at us.

"You can't do this," he says, gesturing at the three of us. "You've got bright careers in front of you. The amount of money you're about to make on this case alone could buy you a Lamborghini."

I just laugh.

"I don't need another car," I say.

"She's just some secretary!" Paul shouts.

The words are barely out of his mouth before I'm leaning across his desk toward him, my face in his, snarling.

"You're wrong," I growl.

Paul stands his ground, but just barely.

"I love her," I say, my voice low and dangerous. "Lawson loves her. She loves us, and that's worth more than anything with a price tag."

Paul gulps audibly.

"I didn't mean—"

I whirl around, offer my hand to Jenna. She takes it tentatively, tears still in her eyes.

"Jenna, I love you, and I'm not going to stop," I tell her.

"I love you too," she whispers. "Kade, Lawson, I'm so sorry—"

I just laugh, and Lawson grins.

"Fuck this place," he says. "Want to get out of here, peach?"

She looks from him to me and then to Paul, who's still standing behind his desk, clearly not sure what's happening.

"Well, I mean, yes, but—"

"How would you like a job at the law offices of Marshall and Chandler?" he asks, glancing up at me.

"Oh, fellas, come on—" Paul starts.

"I think it should be Chandler and Marshall," I say, a grin spreading across my face.

Jenna just laughs, and she's still laughing when the three of us leave Paul's office. We don't even get our things, we just leave.

It feels good. It feels *amazing* to finally admit what we've been hiding all this time, and as we make our way to the elevator, I feel a lightness I haven't felt in ages.

CHAPTER TWENTY-EIGHT

JENNA

I CAN'T BELIEVE THAT JUST HAPPENED.

The whole taxi ride home — or, to Lawson's place, which has more or less become my home in the past few weeks — I'm reeling with what just happened.

That was crazy. It was reckless of them *and* reckless of me — I just walked away from a perfectly good job because one of my boyfriends said he was going to start a law firm.

I know I should be more worried than I am. *Way* more worried, because all I've got is their word that I'll be okay and land on my feet, but honestly?

That's enough.

I trust Lawson and Kade with my life, more than anything. I know they'd never do anything to hurt me, or anything that might really endanger me.

As soon as we get to Lawson's condo, he walks to his huge kitchen, opens the fridge, and pulls out a bottle of Dom Perignon, waving it at Kade and me and grinning.

We're still standing in his living area, our jackets still on, and there's a loud *pop!* as Lawson opens the champagne, the cork bouncing off his ceiling.

Kade frowns slightly as he pulls his tie off, tossing it over the back of a chair.

"What's that for?" he asks.

"Are you serious?" asks Lawson, already pulling champagne flutes down from a cabinet.

"Well, we just quit our jobs very dramatically and don't have a backup plan," Kade points out, his voice gruff, his arms folded over his chest.

Lawson raises one eyebrow at us, smirking.

"We've been talking about this for ages," he says.

"That's not the same as a plan."

Lawson picks up all three flutes and brings them over to us, an unmistakable swagger in his stride. He gives one first to me, then raises both his eyebrows before offering one to Kade.

"You're sure you deserve this?" he asks, laughing.

"Give me that," Kade says, and takes the glass from Lawson. "I didn't say it wasn't a good thing."

This whole time I've been quiet. I think it's a good thing, and I do trust them, but the reality of what just happened is really starting to sink in.

"Jenna?" Lawson asks softly. "You all right?"

I stare into the bubbles rising through my champagne and try to corral my thoughts into some sort of neat, orderly line.

"I'm all right," I say slowly, still watching the bubbles. "It's just... it's a lot to take in, you know?"

"We'll take care of you," Kade suddenly says.

His eyes are piercing right through me, serious and dark, and I nod, warmth spreading through me.

"I know," I say quietly, and then smile. "But still, that was quite a day."

Lawson looks at Kade.

Kade looks at Lawson, and for a moment, they share a significant *look* at each other.

"What?" I ask.

"Nothing. Shall we toast? To our new law firm and newest employee!"

We clink glasses together and each drink, but I'm still suspicious. They're still giving each other that *significant* look, and I'm even more suspicious.

"Tell me," I order them in my sternest voice. I put one hand on my hip and stand up straight, even though I'm easily half a foot shorter than either of them.

"Okay, okay," Kade mutters. "You tell her."

"It was your idea," Lawson counters.

"Tell me now!" I command. I even stomp one foot.

"We bought you a condo," Kade says.

I stop. I stare at both of them in turn, wondering if I misheard.

Then I slam the rest of my champagne, not caring *how* expensive it was.

"A condo?" I ask, slightly reeling.

That is pure insanity, buying real estate in New York City.

"It's on the top floor of a building on the upper east side," Lawson says. "You can see Central Park from the eastern windows."

My mouth is hanging open.

"To be honest, we didn't exactly buy it for you," Kade says. He's smiling now, a mischievous light in his eyes.

"Okay," I say, because I've got *no* clue what to say to all this.

"We bought it for *us*," Lawson says, throwing Kade a quick look. "We didn't want to tell you yet, because it needs some fixing up and we just wanted to take you there and let you see it."

I swallow hard, putting my glass down on a side table. Something is welling up in my chest — gratitude, love, disbelief that my life is suddenly going like this.

"You guys bought a condo so we could all live together?" I ask, my voice whispery with tears.

"There's another reason we didn't want to tell you yet,"

Lawson says, shooting Kade a look. "We don't want to just move in with you, Jenna. We want you to be ours forever."

I swallow against the lump in my throat.

"Where is it?" Kade asks Lawson. Lawson walks over to a desk on one side of the room and comes back with a small black box.

My knees nearly give out. My head is swirling. My hands start shaking as both of them get down on one knee.

"Marry us," Kade says, his voice suddenly soft and gentle. "Please."

"Jenna, we both fell for you the minute we saw you walk into our office," Lawson says. "I know it's unconventional, but will you marry us?"

I'm frozen. I thought this was insanity before, but that was after I'd only quit my job, and *before* my boyfriends told me that they'd bought a condo for the three of us and *then* proposed. My heart is pounding and my hands are shaking, and I know I have to answer them but I'm so shaken that I can't think of the right words to say.

But then I look at them. For once, I look down into their eyes — light and dark — and I see it. I see love and trust and utter devotion, that these two men want to give me everything for the rest of their lives.

And in that moment, I know. I know beyond a shadow of a doubt that what I'm about to do is the right thing.

"Yes," I say, my voice shaking.

Lawson grins his easy grin, slipping the ring onto my finger. It's beautiful, an ornate white gold band with one large diamond surrounded by two slightly smaller ones.

"That's the three of us," Kade explains, his voice gruff again.

"I love it," I whisper.

"We don't really know what to do, legally speaking," he goes on. "But we'll figure something out."

"We are lawyers, after all," Lawson says drily.

They stand. I'm still staring at the ring in utter shock, totally unable to get my head around what just happened.

Okay, so I quit my job.

And now I have a condo. Apparently.

And now I'm also getting married.

That last thought makes me grin, and as Lawson and Kade stand, I start laughing, looking up into their faces. Kade looks wryly amused, but Lawson laughs back at me, joy glinting in his eyes.

"Is that enough for you today, or can you handle any more?" he asks, winking.

The question sobers me immediately.

"Why? What else? You're not going to tell me that—"

"I was being lascivious, peach," he says, taking me in his arms. He slides one hand down my back until he's grabbed my ass and given it a nice, firm squeeze.

Suddenly, all my nerves have turned to heat, and they're flowing through my body like liquid fire.

"Because we've got two more things you're going to handle before the night is over," he says, his voice bottoming out.

THE CHAMPAGNE IS ALREADY GOING to my head as I kiss Lawson deeply, his tongue already in my mouth, his hands already all over me. The ring on my finger sparkles in the light of sunset through his condo's huge windows, my hand on his strong shoulder.

"The condo was my idea," Kade's voice says, right in my ear, close enough that his lips brush the outer shell and send shivers down my spine. "I should get some credit too, you know."

I turn away from Lawson and instantly Kade captures my mouth with his. Someone's hands are meandering over my chest, palming both my breasts at once through my shirt and bra.

Kade's thick cock is hard against my ass, and on my other side, Lawson's hard against my belly.

I'm trapped in the best possible way.

"Think you can handle one more round today, peach?" Kade growls in my ear as he slides one hand up my thigh, pushing my skirt up over my hips. "I know you left your panties somewhere else already."

I blush hard, even as I'm gasping for breath, but Lawson just chuckles.

"When we've got our own firm we won't have to take turns anymore," he says. "Besides, you can't be jealous. I know about the supply closet yesterday."

Now it's Kade's turn to chuckle deeply, his fingers already against the wetness between my legs.

"You're more than ready for another round," he says, his other hand tightening on my waist. "You're practically begging for it."

I moan quietly, bucking my hips back against him, because he's right. I'm already throbbing with desire for both of them, my skirt hiked around my waist. I want them *right* here, *right* now — but I have a bad feeling they're not going to give it to me, not yet.

"Take me," I whimper. "Just bend me over the couch and fuck me, *please*."

Kade's finger slides deeper into me, and it's joined by a second. Lawson's lips are on my throat, his hands making quick work of the buttons on my blouse.

"I love it when you talk dirty, peach," Kade murmurs into my ear, his fingers in my pussy twisting against my pleasure spots. "It's my favorite sound in the world."

"Beautiful," Lawson agrees. He's unhooked my bra and now it's loose over my chest, so he pushes it out of the way, closing his lips around one nipple.

More fingers slide into my pussy. My eyes fly open as I gasp, realizing that they belong to Lawson, as he crooks them against my sensitive inner wall, making me moan yet again, with desire and lust and some kind of deep satisfaction that I can't quite name.

I've got them both inside me at once, the most satisfying feeling I know. I practically melt into their arms, hooking one leg mindlessly around Lawson as he lavishes my nipples with attention.

"It feels so good when you're both inside me," I murmur.

Behind me, there's a hitch in Kade's breathing, and then his other hand grabs me even more roughly, pulling me back against him.

"Good," he says.

Without saying anything else, suddenly he lifts me, both of them pulling their fingers out. He carries me through the living room and into his bedroom, tossing me onto his enormous king-sized bed. The windows here look out over New York City, and the sunset tonight is gorgeous.

Then, Kade's on top of me, pushing my legs apart with one knee. His suit jacket and tie are off, but otherwise, he's still fully dressed while I'm half-undressed, my skirt around my hips and my shirt unbuttoned, my bra loose.

Across the room, the fireplace whooshes on. It's remote controlled, and then Lawson is on the bed too, jacket and tie off.

Kade yanks on my skirt, trying to pull it down, while Lawson slides one hand under my disheveled bra, lightly playing with a nipple. I arch my back toward him and he chuckles, doing the same with his other hand.

"—hate this skirt—" Kade mutters.

"It zips," Lawson offers, bending down to claim my mouth, lavishing his attention on me. I moan into him, writhing as Kade finally reaches behind me, unzips my skirt, and tugs it off.

"I don't see why you can't wear something easier to get off you," he says, his mouth against my stomach, my leg around his torso. "Or maybe nothing at all."

"Well, we are starting our own firm," Lawson says, still lazily caressing my nipples. "Maybe we'll have *very* casual Fridays."

Kade yanks my legs even further apart, his hands rough on the soft skin of my inner thighs. Now his mouth is on the place where my hip meets my thigh, and he licks and nibbles around it until his lips are nearly on mine, teasing and tantalizing me.

"We could have casual every day," he says, his voice low and raspy with desire. "Take plenty of *very* long lunches."

With that he gives me a long, slow lick, the tip of his tongue traveling from the bottom of my slit all the way up to my clit, where he flicks me lightly a few times, making me shudder. I moan explosively, my legs jerking tighter around his body, but he doesn't react at all.

He just does it again.

"Kade," I gasp. "That feels so good."

Lawson growls, kissing me harder, his hands now rough on my breasts. I lock my hands into his hair and pull him down against me, hard, Kade's tongue still ravishing me.

Even though he started out slow, he gets harder and faster almost immediately. Before I know it his hands are pushing my legs apart, pinning me down as he licks me again and again.

It doesn't take long before I'm losing control, moaning their names out loud. I can't stop begging him to take me, fuck me, but he doesn't. He just licks and sucks me until I'm coming hard, moaning into Lawson's mouth as my whole body jerks with pleasure.

But even as the feeling washes over and then fades, slowly, I know that's just the beginning. I haven't even stopped coming yet when Lawson pulls back and suddenly Kade pulls me out of my shirt and bra, then flips me over, pushing me to my hands and knees.

Lawson's already undoing his belt, right in front my face. I can see the outline of his huge, hard cock below his gray suit pants, and I swear my mouth is watering for it.

But he tortures me, just a little. He takes his time unbuckling, then unzipping, so by the time it springs out I'm breathless with anticipation as he gives himself one hard, long stroke from root to tip.

I reach out and put my hand on it, forcing myself not to moan as I do. My whole body is quivering with anticipation, the rock-hard flesh in my hand reminding me of how *good* it feels when he fucks me with it.

Then Kade is back on me again, his tongue in my pussy before I'm even recovered. I groan as he licks me hard and fast again, my breath coming quickly. He's still licking as he slides his fingers along my slit and pushes them inside me, working my sensitive inner wall.

I push my hips back, one hand still wrapped around Lawson's cock, and as I do, I open my mouth and suck in Lawson's tip. He growls above me, his hand on my hand, sending a quick spasm of excitement through my body.

"This is my second-favorite sight," he murmurs.

I slide my lips down his shaft, forcing myself to take my time.

"I'll tell you my first favorite later tonight," he promises, his eyes closing with pleasure. "Since I'm going to be seeing it."

I think I know what he's talking about, and I swear my whole body jolts with anticipation, like I've touched a live wire. Just as Lawson hits the back of my throat, I feel Kade's tongue again. He's slowly making his way down, past where his fingers are working my pussy, to my back hole.

My eyes widen. He's never done this before, not with his tongue — his fingers and cock, sure, but *this* is new and dirty and completely...

He circles the tight bud with his tongue and I moan, my voice reverberating through Lawson's cock and making him exhale hard, his fingers tightening in my hair.

Fuck, I like this. It's dirty as hell and I can't believe how *much* I like it, but I do.

At last I relax my throat and swallow Lawson, the loud groan coming from his chest telling me just how much he likes it when I do this. The three of us start moving together in the harmony we've perfected, back and forth and up and down.

There's no denying that I'm going to come again. I never could hold out against the two of them, and they know it. Kade works me harder and harder, his fingers and tongue moving while I bob and up down on Lawson's cock, listening to him groan.

Finally, I can't hold out any more. I come hard with Lawson's cock still down my throat, Kade's fingers in my pussy and his tongue in my ass, giving me pleasures I hadn't known existed until now.

I'm shaking when I finish, my arms and legs barely able to hold me up on my hands and knees. Lawson pulls his cock from my mouth and leans down, kissing me deeply, one hand on my chin.

"I love you," he says softly.

I swallow hard, panting for breath.

"I love you too," I whisper.

Now Kade's behind me, his big body arched over mine, and he gently pulls my head back, angling my mouth so he can kiss me.

"And I love you," he murmurs.

"I love both of you," I answer, still a little lost in my own delirium.

Then Lawson is on his back, Kade behind me. He lifts me gently until I'm straddling Lawson, his cock pointing straight up toward the ceiling. Even now I marvel at its size, so thick I can barely get my hand around it.

"You know what we're going to do tonight?" Kade asks, his voice deep and gravelly in my ear.

I bite my lip as he pushes me forward, his length solid against my lower back, making me ache.

"What?" I ask, even though I've got a pretty good idea.

"We're going to fuck you together," he goes on, his voice sweet and husky in my ear.

I swear, every nerve in my body crackles at that sentence.

"We can't wait any more, peach," Lawson says, his hands tweaking both my nipples at once as I kneel over him on my hands and knees. "I want to feel you come on my cock while I'm deep in your pussy and Kade is buried in your ass."

Kade nudges the head of his cock against my slippery lower lips, and I moan out loud, totally unable to control myself. I'm still nervous about the thought of taking them both at once — they're *huge*, is that even possible? — but the mere thought of is making my pussy practically drip in anticipation.

"Take me," I manage to gasp out. "Both of you."

Below me, Lawson smiles, a glint in his eye.

"We will, peach," he says softly. "But don't worry, we'll take our time."

He pulls me in for a deep kiss, his mouth opening mine and his tongue invading my mouth, plundering me, his hands still on my nipples. I'm still there, Lawson's mouth on mine, when Kade slides into me from behind.

He hilts himself in one long, slow thrust, and by the time it's over I'm moaning into Lawson's mouth with pleasure, gasping for air. Kade's got both hands on my hips, pulling me back against him, going as deep as he possibly can. I feel powerless and helpless, overtaken with pleasure.

"You like getting fucked by a big cock, don't you, you dirty girl?" Kade says softly.

He pulls out just a little but then sinks back in, a low growl coming from deep in his chest.

"Yes," I manage to gasp out.

Lawson's hand leaves my nipple, traveling south, and in a moment the head of his cock is against my clit, slippery with precum. He massages me with his cock and I shudder again, a slow wave rippling through me.

"Good, because I've got a big cock and I like fucking you," Kade says, just a hint of a smile in his voice.

He keeps fucking me deep and slow. Lawson kisses me sometimes, his cock rubbing against my clit. I'm nearly dizzy with pleasure, spread out and vulnerable for these two men.

Soon, I'm on the edge again, my head against Lawson's shoulder as I moan. Kade doesn't speed up or fuck me harder, just keeps hitting every pleasure zone inside me with slow, deep strokes as I gasp and pant.

"Come for us, peach," Lawson murmurs. "One more time."

He rubs my clit a little harder, and at his command I let go, the wave breaking over me. I cry out into his shoulder, my whole body rocking and jerking.

The moment it's over Kade stops, his breathing fast and hard, like he's trying to collect himself. He slides his hands up and then down my spine, then pulls out.

At the same moment he takes me by one shoulder and lifts me up to kneeling and before I know it, Lawson's cock is right there, at my center, the head already between my lips, Kade steadying me from behind.

I sink onto it, savoring the rush of pleasure even as my last orgasm is still rocking through my core. Lawson growls, grasping my hips in his hands and moving me back and forth.

He grins.

"I love it when you ride my cock," he says, tracing one nipple with a fingertip. "Use me for pleasure any time, baby."

I lean forward slightly, my hands on his chest, moving myself up and down on him slowly. I feel like all my nerves are sensitized and if I go too hard or too fast I might come again, and I don't know how many more times I can come before my joints simply rattle apart.

Kade kisses the back of my neck, one hand coming around, snaking two fingers around a nipple and pinching.

I gasp, arching my back. I'm a little nervous about what happens next, but I'm too turned on and too relaxed from coming my brains out to overthink it.

Behind me, there's the sound of a bottle snapping shut and Kade's hand hooks over my shoulder, like he's keeping me in place.

"Ready for both of us?" he whispers in my ear.

I swallow hard and try to relax, my whole body aching with anticipation. I can feel my pussy gripping Lawson's cock tightly, already halfway to climax.

"I'm ready," I whisper back.

Kade pushes me forward, my hands on Lawson's shoulders. Now the tip of his cock is against my tightly puckered back entrance, slippery as he circles me slowly.

Then he's inside me, just the tip. My eyes fly open and my hands tighten on Lawson's shoulders as Kade pushes himself in, a millimeter at a time, stretching me and filling me completely.

"Relax," Lawson whispers, and I let my hands go slack. Kade slides in another few millimeters, and this time, I push back. I take Lawson up to the hilt and I hear Kade's breath hiss between his teeth as he opens me up.

I stop, catching my breath and swallowing hard. This is like nothing I've ever done or experienced before — it feels impossible, like there's no more room inside my body, but I've never wanted anything more.

I want them. I *need* them to claim me together, make me theirs in this crazy, impossible way.

Kade slides in again and suddenly I feel a slight *pop* as the ring of muscle lets the head of his cock through. I don't think I can move, I'm so stuffed full, and he groans into my ear.

"You like being stuffed full of two cocks?" he asks, his voice thick and raspy as he pushes into me.

I can only grunt as Kade slides deeper, faster now. My whole body shudders and shakes, an icy wave crashing over me.

"Good," is the only word I can manage to moan out as Kade hilts himself in my ass. Even though he's being gentle it feels rough — both big cocks fully inside me, bottoming out.

They start moving, and all I can do is hang on. Spasms wrack through my body as they find a rhythm together, my eyes rolling back into my head as they share pleasure spots and make me theirs again and again.

I can't stop coming. I can barely control my own body. I think I'm moaning, maybe screaming with pleasure, but I know that I'm completely at the mercy of the two men inside me, under me, holding me up.

I have no idea how long we fuck for. It could be thirty seconds or thirty minutes, but then Lawson is growling *I'm gonna come, I can't last like this* at me though gritted teeth and I'm begging him to come inside me. I'm begging them *both* to come inside and fill me up, and Kade grabs me roughly, pinning me against his body, and together they both drive deep into me.

I don't know who comes first, but I come one last time as they do, feeling like I'm breaking into a thousand pieces as their cocks jerk in unison, spilling their seed together. Kade's got one hand hooked around my shoulder, Lawson's holding up my torso with one arm and holding my hand with the other, our fingers interlaced.

After we come together there's a long, long pause. I lean into them, my men, closing my eyes, and I feel at home. I feel like, of all the places, this is exactly where I'm supposed to be and who I'm supposed to be with.

CHAPTER TWENTY-NINE

JENNA

I STAND UP FROM MY DESK AND STRETCH, TRYING TO REACH THE ceiling with my fingertips. I've been sitting in this chair all morning, and even though it was expensive, I'm beginning to realize it's a terrible chair.

I put *get self new office chair* on my mental to-do list. It's not the first item on the list. It's not even the fortieth item on the list.

"Now bend over," a slow, deep voice says behind me.

"This is workplace harassment," I tease. "I should go to Human Resources."

"I've got a feeling you'd win that case, given that you *are* Human Resources," Lawson says.

I'm also the executive assistant, director of marketing, the office manager... you get the idea.

"So if I fire you from your own firm, then what?" I ask, turning around and leaning against my desk.

"Then I imagine you're *also* out of a job, given that you work for me," he says. "But maybe I could talk you out of going to Human Resources with that complaint. Your back bothering you again?"

I nod, standing up straight and arching.

"You need a new chair. Turn around," he orders me, and I do, bracing my hands against my desk.

Lawson takes me by the hips, his strong thumbs digging into the knot of muscle at the base of my spine.

"Unnh," I say, the sound slipping out by accident.

He just chuckles quietly behind me.

"That good?" he asks.

His voice goes raspy, and I swallow hard as his fingers work my back.

"Harder," I say. It comes out louder than I mean it to, and now Lawson *growls*.

We're out in our new office's main space, meaning anyone in the office building's hallway could come in through our door and catch Lawson bending me over my desk for a *very* hands-on backrub.

Not that it would matter. It's their firm now, they can do anything they like and they're not about to fire themselves for giving their girlfriend backrubs.

I can feel my back relaxing as Lawson digs into me, and he steps closer. *Now* I can feel the thick ridge of his cock between my buttocks, and instantly, my body pulses with desire.

"Is *that* better?" he asks, his voice bottoming out.

"Almost," I say, pushing my hips back against him, back pain forgotten. "But you know what would really help?"

Lawson doesn't answer, just shoves my skirt up roughly until it's around my hips and bends me over the desk. He groans when he sees I'm not wearing panties — I stopped bothering.

"Jesus, peach," he says. "How am I supposed to ever get work done when I know you're out here like this?"

I'm about to tell him that's not *my* problem when the other office door opens and Kade steps through, his suit jacket off and his shirt sleeves rolled up. He takes in what's going on for a long moment, smirking.

"You didn't know she stopped wearing panties?" he asks Lawson.

"I guess I'm behind on office gossip," Lawson answers.

Kade saunters over slowly until he's across my desk from me and he leans in, giving me a long kiss.

"My lunch meeting just canceled," he says, his voice wicked. "And it looks like the two of you are free."

We have a working lunch, right there on my desk. I come three times.

God, I love my job.

EPILOGUE

JENNA

One Year Later

"Is it a boy or a girl?" the saleswoman asks briskly, glancing at my huge belly.

I put one hand on it, protectively. It's not because of her, it's just a habit I've acquired.

"Girl," Kade answers before I can. "Penelope."

"I thought we weren't telling people," Lawson says, one eyebrow raised.

Kade smiles. He's been doing that a lot more lately, and he's got one hand protectively on my back.

"Sorry, I'm just excited," he says.

The saleswoman at the Bananas in the City Baby Boutique smiles neutrally, but I can tell she's not quite sure what to make of us. I'm sure she gets mostly couples in here, looking to put together a baby registry, but when it's three people?

All wearing matching wedding bands?

And all acting *very* hands-on?

I can only imagine what she must think. Luckily, I don't really care.

"Well, we have a wonderful selection of girls' clothing," she says. "And, of course, we're happy to monogram anything that you buy free of charge, as long as you give us a couple of days' notice. In fact, right now it's very popular with new parents to monogram their babies' bedsheets, it really gives the nursery that *finished* feel…"

~

HALF AN HOUR LATER, we're finally rid of the saleswoman, though she did leave us with the scanner gun so we can add things to the registry. It's my first time doing this — we got married in a very small ceremony in a park, with only our families present. We thought our arrangement was too non-traditional for a big celebration.

But a baby? Everyone wants to celebrate a baby.

Kade is examining a car seat-and-stroller combo like it's the latest Supreme Court decision, crouching down in front of it and frowning.

"This says it has six different positions," he says, sounding mystified. "How many ways can you put a baby in a stroller?"

"Upside-down, maybe?" Lawson suggests. "I've heard it's good for… I don't know, development?"

I sigh dramatically and pat my belly.

"I promise not to let them cart you around upside-down," I tell my bump.

"Well, if the stroller offers it, why not?" Lawson teases.

"Seriously, this is more complicated than our office chairs," Kade says. "And those practically require a Ph.D. to operate."

"If we can even get the baby home from the hospital I'll consider it a win," Lawson says. "According to this *suggested baby items* sheet, we need an 'on the go' stroller and an 'around the neighborhood' stroller, not to mention a bassinet *and* a crib and something called a pack-n-play—"

I put one hand on Lawson's arm, trying to soothe him.

"Lawson, it'll be fine," I assure him. "People have been having babies without any of that stuff for millions of years, don't let it stress you out."

He sighs.

"I know," he says, stepping closer and putting an arm around my shoulders. "It's just… I want to do it right, you know?"

I nestle into him.

"You will," I say. "I'm sure of it."

"You can't possibly be more lost than me," Kade offers, still standing with the stroller. "I don't even know how many children this thing is supposed to hold. It might be two?"

Lawson chuckles.

"Any surprise twins in there?" he asks me, one hand on my belly.

Penelope kicks his hand, and he grins.

"There had better not be," I tease. "I think one is all we can handle."

"It might be worth getting it if we're going to have another one pretty soon," Kade says, glancing over at us.

Both of them glance over at me, then freeze at the look on my face.

"I spent eighteen weeks getting nauseous every time I turned around, and the moment that ended my ankles swelled up and now I can't even roll myself over in bed," I say. "Now is *not* the time to ask if we're going to have a soccer team's worth of children."

Kade grins and stands, walking over to me.

"A soccer team would be ludicrous," he says, kissing me gently on the head while he caresses my belly softly. "I was thinking more along the lines of basketball."

I raise one eyebrow at Lawson, and he holds up five fingers.

"We'll see how cute this one is before I make any more decisions," I say, and Penelope kicks me again.

The idea of being pregnant four more times doesn't really appeal to me. I'm only at thirty-two weeks, and I already feel like I barely remember a life where I could walk between parked cars.

But the thought of Lawson and Kade taking our kids to a museum and looking at dinosaur bones? Or the thought of them on the couch during movie night, our children using them as climbing equipment while they eat popcorn?

That could just about convince me.

"She'll be cute," Lawson assures me. "She'll be beautiful, just like her mom."

He wraps his arms around me from behind, planting a kiss on the top of my head.

"If she's all we have, we'd still be lucky," Kade says, leaning in for a kiss. "Just like we're lucky to have you."

Another couple shopping for strollers give us a weird look, but I don't care. I'm here with both my husbands and our unborn baby, and everything is just about perfect.

Is it conventional? Not at all.

But am I blissfully happy?

Absolutely.

That night, after we finish making a baby registry and Kade puzzles over the mechanics of car seats, we go back to the condo we all share. Lawson makes us lamb chops for dinner while I sit on the couch, drinking tea while Kade rubs my swollen feet.

When we go to bed I'm nestled in the middle of them, just like always. They kiss me one by one, wrapping me in their strong arms before we all drift off to sleep.

"Love you," Kade says.

"Love you, peach," Lawson says.

I smile into the dark as Penelope kicks me again.

"I love you too," I say.

THE END

ABOUT PARKER

I write obsessed, dominant, alpha heroes who stop at *nothing* to get their women - and get them dirty!

I can be found driving around my small, southern town in either my minivan or hubby's pickup truck. No one here is the wiser about my secret writing life... and I definitely prefer it that way!

www.parkergreyromance.com
parker@parkergreyromance.com

Made in the USA
Las Vegas, NV
03 March 2024

86650978R10104